STEPPING INTO THE STORM

A frontline CRNA's experience
battling a novel virus pandemic in Detroit

by Tori Rose, MS, CRNA

The following material is the intellectual property of the author and may not be reproduced or shared in any way without express written confirmation from the author. Author's views and opinions are their own and do not in any way reflect the thoughts or opinions of any hospital or other medical professionals within the Michigan healthcare system unless specifically stated.

Courage transforms fear into determination. It is embracing life fully, without holding back, doing what must be done even if it is difficult or risky. When we are tempted to give up, courage supports us to take the next step. It allows us to face adversity with confidence. Courage opens us to new possibilities and gives us strength to sacrifice for what we love. Courage gives me the strength to make this journey with all my heart.

— THE VIRTUES PROJECT

TABLE OF CONTENTS

Foreword
Prologue
Chapter 1
Chapter 2
Chapter 3
Chapter 4
Chapter 5
Chapter 6
Chapter 7
Chapter 8
Chapter 9
Chapter 10
Chapter 11
Chapter 12
Chapter 13
Chapter 14
Chapter 15
Afterword

FOREWORD

I am a clinician, not a writer. I'm not as eloquent as I would like to be. I am not political, I don't know very much about the ins and outs of our economy and I'm not well versed in the administrative/budget side of hospitals.

This is my first-hand account of a highly unusual and unprecedented scenario. I have quite literally put blood, sweat and tears into this project and experience as you will read.

I first have to thank my Lord and savior Jesus Christ for so much, including his protection during this fearful time.

I want to thank my husband for his undying support. His calm demeanor and confidence in me has carried me through some very dark days. His encouragement when I needed it most regularly centered me and helped keep me out of a lasting depression.

His extra work around the house and with our beloved children when I was busy writing this book or too distracted from stress will never be forgotten. He is my forever rock solid foundation.

Thank you to my incredible family for your love and support. I also have some good friends to thank for their support (and flowers, cards and gifts): They know who they are. An extra special thank you to the good friend who hosted me in her home for her hospitality and much needed support.

I also want to thank my prized friend, Dawn, for her literary magic on this project. Without her, I wouldn't have taken this leap and had the confidence to see this project through. I am forever grateful for her hard work, brilliant brain and encouragement.

The following is based on actual true events and scenarios. This is a memoir of my time spent caring for patients during the surge of a new and unknown virus that will be referred to as the NOVA virus, or NOVA, for the duration of this manuscript.

I'd like to start by explaining the policies of the vast majority of hospitals during this pandemic. In most hospitals, the current policies I have seen do not require a 14-day quarantine when coming into contact with a patient who is confirmed NOVA positive. If this were the case, there would be no one left to care for the sick.

The employees coming into contact with confirmed positive patients are expected to take extra care to monitor their temperature and look for any symptoms but can work if they do not present symptoms. The majority of healthcare workers would never qualify for testing unless they were showing symptoms due to the limited quantities of tests. I personally (and thankfully) never showed any symptoms.

I want to acknowledge all of the first responders and the heroes in the Emergency Rooms (ERs) around the world. They are truly a huge part of the frontline and undertake huge risks. The nurses and workers doing all of the drive-up testing, paramedics and EMTs, ER physicians, nurses and other staff, Respiratory Therapists (RTs), NOVA floor nurses, ICU nurses and nursing assistants, phlebotomists in the lab, supply personnel (the amount of supplies needed to care for one NOVA patient on a ventilator is hugely increased from everyday care, and every patient needs that increased amount), the pharmacy department for working at breakneck speed throughout all hours of the day, X-ray technologists (every NOVA suspect patient needs a chest X-ray, and they are right next to the patients to obtain an X-ray!) and many more are real-life heroes. There are many other thankless but essential behind-the-scenes people who make the system run and I acknowledge and thank them all for their service and bravery.

I also want to acknowledge and thank some businesses for their support of healthcare providers during these difficult times. Some that I know of are: The Marriott in Detroit, for offering free rooms for healthcare workers, the Hilton, who partnered with American Express to donate 1 million hotel nights to frontline medical professionals, Biggby Coffee and Starbucks for providing free coffee to show us love and support, Crocs for donating a free pair of shoes, The North Face for giving a 50% discount to healthcare workers in the U.S., Taco Bell for offering meals at half off and many McDonald's locations for offering free "Thank You Meals" to us as well. These things make me a loyal customer, and I'm grateful for their gratitude and generosity.

I have never been diagnosed with Post Traumatic Stress Disorder (PTSD), nor do I take it lightly. I hold our veterans in the highest regard and am forever grateful for their services and sacrifices. I have not, nor will I ever, compare my days during this crisis with their trauma. I simply use it as a point of reference, as I was deeply affected and had lasting questions of whether my life was in danger outside of the actual events related to contracting the virus.

I know there is a very real problem with obtaining and supplying PPE (Personal Protective Equipment) in some places in America. I do not minimize the severity and horrible situation this is for our precious healthcare workers. We all have the right to be protected to the highest levels. The following is a snapshot of my two shifts and what I experienced. I know that in China, and even Italy and France, they have seemingly safer and more plentiful PPE.

A lot of our PPE is made in China and has been used up by those who had the virus outbreak first overseas, plus the supply is down to critical levels since those factories that make PPE were forced to shut down due to NOVA repercussions.

I foresee the U.S. making great changes moving forward to diversify our supply chain and potentially create these products within our own borders.

This is meant to be informative, but not have every statistic researched. A lot of the stats are hearsay and based off of best guesses and/or stated opinions at the time. The NOVA situation is so fluid. New information and recommendations come out daily. By the time my words hit the screen, some of the numbers and ideas may be obsolete, outdated or found to be ineffective. The tone of the book is a snapshot in time.

Some details have been altered to protect the privacy of patients and institutions.

PROLOGUE

In front of me hangs a sign announcing that I'll have to make my way through the ER in order to leave the hospital for the day.

Gulp.

The ER seems like the absolute last place on earth I want to be right now, but all of the other exits are locked down and clearly blocked with bright yellow "CAUTION: DO NOT CROSS" tape like at a crime scene, so I have no choice. The hospital isn't allowing anyone into the building without first being screened, and the staffing is reduced at night, leaving just the one entry and exit for the entire building.

Deep breath and hold it. It'll be OK. I'm almost out of here.

I have to be buzzed into the ER because it's locked from the rest of the hospital as are most ERs, for standard security measures. As the door swings open to the ER waiting area, I'm surprised at how dark it is on the other side. Everywhere I look, people are wearing facemasks, and they're not hospital workers, but potential patients waiting to be examined and their rides. The small space is so crowded with people and wheelchairs.

I start running. I'm not wearing a mask, leaving me fully susceptible to catching what these people have if I'm too near. The tight quarters feel suffocating. It's terrifying; something like out of a horror movie. I'm fully expecting the lights to flicker like they would in a slasher film, and a monster to step out from the shadows.

Except in this horror movie, the monster is all around me.

I want out as fast as I can. I run while holding my breath; a hard task.

How on earth did I get here?

A few weeks ago, I was a nurse anesthetist who provided most of her care on elective (read: non life-threatening) surgeries that are scheduled ahead of time. Every surgery is serious, yes, but before this shift, there was an element of calm control that definitely does not exist anywhere around me today.

Here I am, long, brown hair still dripping down my back where I'd carefully tucked it into the back of my raggedy old random shirt from my post-shift shower, sprinting through an ER in Detroit.

I'm not wearing underwear, I've got an old coat on with the hood up and I'm carrying a garbage bag of my belongings that swings beside me as I dodge people in masks in an attempt to make it outside before I have to take a breath.

I am the star of this movie, only there is no camera and no director. I want to scream and cry at the same time. This is chaos, this is horrifying, and this is my life now.

Finally, I reach the exit door, plow past two security guards and continue the mad dash to my car, hitting the "unlock" button on my key fob a few more times than is probably necessary once it comes into view. I barely look for cars as I sprint across the road to the parking lot. I glance around as I sprint, struck almost funny as the image of Eminem from the movie 8 Mile flits through my frantic brain. Right city, wrong theme.

Finally, I'm there. The 90-second run has left me breathless; my heart is pounding.

Once inside, I lock the doors and turn the key, my mind buzzing with all I'd seen and done in the past 14 hours. I have never wanted to be home more in my life.

CHAPTER 1

Tuesday, 6:35 p.m.

I am carefree and cooking dinner after a day off of work. I'm enjoying the sunshine coming through the windows. My children are outside on their swing set for one of the first times of the year; it's a rare occurrence in northern Ohio that is fighting off the effects of winter, and even though temps were only in the high 40s, it was a cheerful day outside.

I smile as I see my husband pushing the baby on the swing, the latter kicking and squealing with delight. There is a lot of happy yelling going on, as is the usual case with my wild kids. I'm expecting to have the next few days off, and as I cook dinner, I run over my schedule for the upcoming day in my head.

Organizing the house was at the top of the list as I plan all I want to do with this unusual extra time off. The children's playroom is a disaster area. They have been out of school for almost two full weeks, ever since the governor shut down all schools. Being cooped up inside leads to an overwhelming amount of toys being played with and not put away. I start to think about how we are going to make them clean up after themselves more now. They are getting older now and can start to learn some responsibility.

I've got some free time to teach them, as I am a Certified Registered Nurse Anesthetist, or CRNA, and with the governor's orders to stop all elective surgeries as an attempt to control the recent NOVA virus) outbreak, there isn't a need for anywhere near the normal number of anesthesia providers in my surrounding cities.

CRNAs are masters- and doctoral-degree prepared advanced practice Registered Nurses who provide anesthetics to patients in every practice setting, and for every type of surgery or procedure. They are the only providers of anesthesia in almost all rural hospitals and the main provider to the men and women in the U.S. Armed Forces.

We were also the first providers dedicated to the specialty of anesthesia, originating all the way back to the 1800s. We practice with a high degree of autonomy and professional respect. I love my job, and it is so rewarding — to be able to drop off a patient to the recovery area after a surgery they wouldn't have otherwise been able to handle without the miracle of anesthesia, knowing they are comfortable and so relieved it's over — it is an amazing feeling.

By choice, I have a unique working situation. I am not employed full-time anywhere but am part-time and per diem (casual or contingent status) at multiple hospitals and surgery centers in the area.

For me, the advantage of being able to work part-time hours so I can be present in my young children's lives far outweighs the comfort of working a set schedule, and I really enjoy the work/life challenge of balancing my professional duties with being a wife and mother. It's truly the best of both worlds.

A career in anesthesia can offer a unique sort of employment setup, as often, a group is contracted to provide the anesthesia services for a hospital or center instead of the providers working directly for the hospital. These groups can provide coverage all over the nation and often service multiple sites within the same state to be able to utilize staff efficiently.

I'm torn from my musings as my cell phone buzzes on the counter next to me. It's a message from one of my employers with a call for help from the Detroit area, about two hours away from where I live.

I knew almost immediately that I would go, nodding my head in agreement as I read the e-mail. Word by word, the initial knee-jerk reaction to lend a hand grew into a firm resolve to do whatever I could.

How could I sit at home and organize my kids' drawers for the next three days when people are dying in the worst pandemic known to our time?

I know I can be a huge help. I have already been reading for weeks about how the effects of the novel NOVA virus could get as bad here, if not worse, as they had in Italy, and I know CRNAs will be called to step up.

It's March 2020, and we are facing a worldwide pandemic unknown to our generation due to a novel, or new, virus which is now referred to as the NOVA virus.

These types of viruses are shaped like a crown and have been around for a very long time. They refer to a group of viruses known to cause respiratory issues. Previous similar viruses included Severe Acute Respiratory Syndrome (SARS) in 2003 and Middle East Respiratory Syndrome (MERS) that surfaced in 2012.

NOVA virus can lead to major health problems, particularly pneumonia and acute respiratory distress syndrome (ARDS), and seems to be the most contagious virus known to this generation. It appears to have started in an animal and passed to humans.

The pandemic has stopped the world in its tracks and caused the U.S. to socially isolate — there are signs and ads everywhere imploring people to stay 6 feet away from everyone, including their own grandparents. This disease has caused more people to have severe breathing problems than anything else, and many hospitals don't have enough ventilators to keep these people alive while they fight the virus and ARDS.

I use ventilators everyday in my role as a CRNA. CRNAs also regularly intubate (skillfully place breathing tubes into a patient's windpipe to assist their breathing) on a daily basis, and are uniquely experienced to help in this situation since we were all ICU RNs before becoming anesthetists. We regularly manage high-risk situations in surgery and our expertise has proven to fill a significant and essential role during this battle.

I remember reading that Italy had recently set age limits on who even qualified to be put on a ventilator because there just weren't enough resources to save everyone. In the beginning, anyone younger than 80 years old qualified, but this virus has spread so quickly that the age had since dropped to 60. This means that for anyone over the age of 60 years, the decision was made before even going to the hospital that you couldn't be saved.

Take a minute and let that sink in. Under those rules, my parents wouldn't qualify for ventilators; neither would my in-laws. Suddenly, this terrifying disease is not only in my country but way too close to home. I didn't know it at the time but in the days ahead, Michigan would regularly hold the number three spot for states hardest hit by the virus.

Ohio and Michigan were within a day or two of each other when issuing stay-at-home orders, school and restaurant closures, etc., yet Michigan would have more than three times the cases and an overwhelming surge to the Detroit hospitals, which made it imperative that they get help from anyone willing. I am licensed in both states, so there isn't a logistical problem to overcome.

Wow. I thought. This is actually happening.

It feels like I am about to go to war. My whole mindset and demeanor change as I call my husband inside to show him the e-mail telling him that I feel I have to help. I know that I could be putting my life in danger, but at the same time I also know it's something

I have to do, and my faith reassures me that God will protect me. I have never felt such a seriousness as I await my husband's response. As usual, he is supportive of me.

"If you feel like you want to go, then you should go," he says in a rare serious tone.

I finish cooking and leave the kitchen in chaos behind me. There are more important things on my mind now than a sink full of dirty dishes. We sit down to dinner. I can't eat, and my mind is racing as I try to seem present with my family, a feeling that would plague me for the next few months.

My husband trusts me and my judgement and can tell that I am determined to help. I can tell he knows this is more serious than any other situation, but he doesn't try to talk me out of it.

We try to make dinner as normal as possible. My husband, bless him, sneaks into the kitchen later that evening and tidies up.

Had I known what was to come, I would have paid more attention to everything. What did the kids talk about at the table? Was the baby still grinning from ear to ear after her afternoon outside? What did we even *have* for dinner?

All of that stuff seems like it happened years ago. It was the last normal night I'm going to have for a while.

After dinner, I called the director who sent the message to ask for more details. There aren't many to give, other than the hospital will take whatever time I can offer; they are very desperate and it's all hands on deck.

I am assured they have plenty of proper personal protective equipment (PPE) and N95 respirators (the tighter-fitting masks that go around the mouth and nose that you have to be fitted for, which make it far less likely to contract an airborne illness).

That helps calm me a little. I've read that there is a severe shortage of PPE across the country and I have major reservations about working in such a contagious environment without safety measures. I wouldn't take that risk for any amount of money.

I fire off a text to my friend from nursing school: She lives near the hospital where I'll be helping out. She invites me to stay with her since her children are out of the house.

I would never stay at another person's house during our state-mandated social isolation, but she works in a hospital setting as well and is equally as exposed to the virus. I'm perplexed by the invitation because her kids are always there, but I take it as another sign that volunteering now is the right decision.

After we spend some time comparing NOVA situations in our respective cities, I call a friend for some advice who has already been reading up on NOVA almost obsessively. She is so serious on the other end as she walks me through the most important times to be vigilant with PPE. She urges me to watch another video on doffing (attentively taking off) the PPE as there are so many crucial points of potential contamination. She asks me what exactly I will be doing there.

"I really don't know," I tell her.

Talking to her was supposed to reassure me — I thought — but instead her tone carries a gravity that only adds to a gnawing feeling in my stomach that I'm about to go to war.

When she ends the call by telling me to take care of myself, it sounds downright ominous.

What have I signed up for?

Armed with all this new information, I have a feeling growing inside of me that my life is about to change. I envision a soldier packing up to go to war, resolved to help but with a healthy fear of the unknown battle ahead.

I gather my worst clothes and shoes with the idea that they will all have to be destroyed after work, and a toothbrush. I never go to work without makeup, but I figure there's no need anymore, plus I don't want to take anything that isn't absolutely essential. Then I sit down to watch the 16-minute video on doffing PPE.

Whoa, it really takes 16 minutes to take this stuff off?

In a family group chat usually reserved for jokes, plans for get-togethers and cheerful celebrations, I reach out for prayers and to tell them where I am heading. I'm in a hurry to get on the road as it's already after 8:30 and it will take nearly two hours to reach my friend's house. Before I left that night, we held a family prayer in my basement.

Right at the end, the baby — she's 18 months old — ran into the middle of us and said her first "Amen!" which brought levity to a very strange time-stopping moment. I hugged my babies tightly and kissed my supportive husband goodbye with tears in my eyes.

I can't wait to see them again. But will I be the same upon my return?

On the drive there, I talk with my host friend, who informed me it was one of the first nights ever that her kids would be staying at their dad's house. I realize that this is a monumental time in a close friend's life too, and it's special that we will be together.

She reassures me that I can stay with her anytime through this crisis, as long as her kids are gone.

At two hours of driving each way and a 12-hour shift between, the commute is way too long to make on a routine basis, but my friend's generous offer makes it so I can bring my own sleeping bag and pillow — to prevent any cross-contamination to her house — and save precious time on the road.

I will leave a bleach wipe trail behind me anywhere I go or touch in her home, too.

My group family text — there are 10 of us in there — blows up with prayers, questions and concerns for my well-being on the ride up. My car has one of those options that reads the texts out loud to me, but I can hardly pay attention to the flood.

I'm either on the phone with my friend I'm about to stay with, praying or wondering what tomorrow will bring, and have a hard time responding via the hands-free technology. One of my "anthem" songs that has been keeping me grounded in my faith and has been on repeat is called *See a Victory* by Elevation Worship. It comes on and one line strikes me hard...

"I'm not backing down from any giant, 'Cause I know how this story ends..." The giant in this case is the virus, and I know my God is in control.

This gives me an overwhelming sense of peace and confidence in the moment.

I know for sure that my mother is freaking out ... that's what my mom does. Per her request, I call my parents to check in as I pull in my friend's driveway around 10:30 p.m.

Just four hours ago, I was cooking dinner in my kitchen and looking forward to the next three days.

My mind is whirling.

My dad answers the phone, and I can hear my mom crying in the background. They want to know what their "baby" is choosing to do, and to get a better understanding of what's going on. Just as every parent wants for their children, my parents want me to sit safely in my home, preferably inside of a bubble, until this nightmare is over.

I put on my "strong" voice and assure them that I won't go into a situation without the proper PPE, and that I feel led to do this. I don't have much information to calm their fears because I really am going into the unknown.

The human mind is such a funny thing. It's at this moment, loud and clear, that Princess Elsa begins belting out "Into the Unknown" in my head. She's been in my head all day and night thanks to my kids, who watched "Frozen II" on a loop during the first few weeks that school was shut down. I had *just* gotten away from that song and yet, here we are again.

Heh.

I chuckle silently at the silliness of the moment during an otherwise nerve-wracking time, then shake my head to clear it as I assure my parents that I will be just fine ... even though I'm not 100 percent sure I believe it myself.

I think they felt better after my call? I shut off the car and head up the driveway, entering my friend's house. It's the first time since I met her more than 20 years ago that we don't hug immediately. This, of course, is due to what we know about the virus and highest potential of transmission at this point, which mandates we "socially distance" each other, 6 feet apart.

I want so badly to comfort her and she wants to reassure me, but this situation makes it impossible to share a heartfelt hug. Still, it's so great to see her. After catching up a bit, I head to bed, knowing I'll need all the energy I can muster to handle what tomorrow throws me. Instead, it's a very restless night, and I get maybe three hours of sleep.

It only gets worse from there.

CHAPTER 2

Wednesday, 6:45 a.m.

Twelve hours after I first received a call for help, I arrive at a hospital I have never seen before, nestled in an unfamiliar suburb of Detroit.

I walk in with my work badge, where I'm met by security and Registered Nurse (RN) screeners, whose job is to question everyone (about potential symptoms and their need to be there) and make sure we sanitize properly. This is standard at all hospitals now.

Everyone inside, and those coming in off the street, are wearing masks; I do not have one and feel ill-equipped. We aren't experiencing this level of outbreak where I live just yet, although it will eventually become common practice there to wear masks everywhere, too.

Well this *is a good start.*

It was different from any other entrance to a hospital I've been to, and I have entered hospitals thousands of times in my almost 20-year career. Per governor's order, no visitors are allowed in the hospital except for the patients in labor, who are allowed one.

There are no volunteers around and no vendors, just those deemed "essential" workers. No gift shops; the coffee shop is closed too. The situation is eerie at best, and downright terrifying if I allow myself to think about it any further.

The only people in this hospital are sick, and just about all of them are confirmed NOVA positive cases. There are also healthy pregnant women here, and I try my best not to think about them being cooped up among so much sadness, terror and death during a time that should be among the happiest in their lives.

Focusing on them will only lead me down a path I'm sure I don't want to — *can't* — go down right now. There are people who need my help.

Starting with the NOVA patients who will be my sole focus during this 12-hour shift.

I meet the director, who rounds up some scrubs and PPE including my size N95 respirator, and shows me to the Post Anesthesia Care Unit (PACU) and operating room (OR) areas that had been transformed into NOVA intensive care units (ICU).

I'm grateful to be able to wear hospital-provided and laundered scrubs in the OR and think about the other nurses who have to wear their own clothes and then take them home to launder. Those people are likely bringing the virus to their homes and into their cars, as the virus can live on clothing for sometime. Overwhelmed days ago, the ICUs are now bursting at the seams.

He proudly tells me that the hospital has installed a negative pressure air removing system for airborne diseases just for this crisis in this OR ICU. In basic terms, this system sucks up the air from the room, preventing it from flowing freely into other areas of the hospital and protecting others from exposure.

The virus is so contagious and said to last three hours in the air. We do our best to attempt to contain it in just the rooms where there are contagious patients, and to the surface of my PPE — the armor that stands between me and the disease — as I enter through the doors.

I later come to realize that, as is the case in most hospitals, there are only a few negative pressure rooms on the other floors. No one ever expected to need them in this many rooms.

There are patients infected all over the hospital, and in places where there aren't negative pressure rooms and the only protection is simply keeping the door closed. I realize I will have to wear my N95 everywhere in the hospital, not just in the patients' rooms. Learning this, the OR is a nice assignment after all and my perspective changes.

I'm also envisioning the pop-up hospitals like the field hospitals in New York City basically made out of tents, or the battleships like the USNS Comfort, and the Cobo Center in Detroit. This disaster throws all rules and regulations out the window, meaning the government is allowing for flexibility to address the urgent need to expand care capacity. It's what is necessary right now.

I arrive at a set of double doors with bright yellow signs on them that announce "DO NOT ENTER" and "NOVA ICU."

Wow. This is ominous.

I meet a few other CRNAs who show me their hospital's anesthesia machines. I'm very familiar with this brand; I use it at two other facilities where I currently work.

These machines are intended to provide anesthetic gases to patients undergoing surgery and have a ventilator component to them, but are not built to be long-term ICU ventilators. They have different features and less therapeutic treatment abilities. They are better than they used to be for sure, but they are not made for the sickest NOVA patients, or for prolonged use, and some patients are being left what we call "on vent" for more than 15 days.

This is unprecedented, but desperate times call for desperate measures. We're all doing the best we can with what we have, and repurposed anesthesia machines are significantly better than nothing at all.

The media is calling for doctors and nurses to even come out of retirement to help. We need all the help we can get; our healthcare workers and systems are already overwhelmed, and this is just the start of it in Michigan. This is a new chapter in our CRNA history, and we are qualified for this scary challenge. Sometimes I wish I weren't qualified ... a desk job working from home sounds mighty fabulous right about now. Definitely safer, anyway.

These newly minted ICUs consist of beds in the PACU and a row of operating rooms along a shared long hallway, a similar setup to basically any other OR department I've seen. The first few ORs already have two patients in each of them.

All of the patients are hooked up to an anesthesia machine that functions as their ventilator because all of the hospital's normal ICU ventilators are already in use. My immediate role is to assist with a new arrival in OR 14, I find out as the patient is about to roll into the unit.

No one told me, or even knows, how many patients could be expected to come behind them. Without warning, my day began to move forward at hyperspeed. As my first patient approaches from down the hall, my heart begins to race as I again feel that my life may never be the same.

Normally I wear my own cute and colorful cloth hats in the OR along with a few items of jewelry. I also have a few pens in my pocket, along with my phone.

Now, I don't wear anything nonessential that I would have to launder at home (my own hats or undershirts), just the disposable bouffant caps. I don't wear jewelry anymore, either.

Will I ever wear jewelry at work again when this is all over? My husband will be disappointed if I don't wear my wedding ring. I will, too. It's a part of me.

My phone is in a clear Ziploc bag and I plan on leaving it in my pocket all day: In fact, it's powered off, and if I had a locker at this facility, it would be in there. I take the time to don (carefully put on) the plastic gown and shoe covers. I make sure everything is secured and fastened. I need every part of me to stay covered to the best of my ability.

I look down.

Dang. I can still see my shoelaces outside of the shoe covers. These shoes are heading straight for the garbage when my shift is over. No chance I'm taking any of this back home with me. My neck and upper chest are also still exposed even with the gown on. I'll be scrubbing my neck raw with soap before I leave this place.

Welp.

Next comes my N95 respirator. I make sure to squeeze the nose piece tightly and make adjustments; this is the most important piece of equipment I've ever needed in my entire life.

I check it one more time as if it is my oxygen tank at the bottom of the ocean and my life depends on it. I then don a regular mask with a plastic face shield over the top of it all to protect my eyes and the N95, followed by two pairs of gloves that I carefully inspect to make sure there are no rips.

My hands are shaking throughout this process and I do my best to swallow back the fear that's bubbling up inside of me.

The respirators are uncomfortable under the best circumstances so I focus on slowing my breathing. In providing an essential barrier between your mouth and the outside world, the respirators also force you to breathe in all of the carbon dioxide you just exhaled, which messes with you on its own after a while, and I don't want to make it even worse.

It's so hot with all of the protection on, and I feel clumsy under all the layers. I'm always cold in the OR, but this pressure-packed moment combined with the protective gear, pushes me to the verge of sweating.

I work again to calm myself as much as possible before my first patient reaches me, but I don't know what I am getting myself into.

Will I have to intubate them?

Intubation is one of the highest-risk moments for transmission of NOVA, as it requires me to have my face within inches of the patient's mouth, where the virus is rampant.

We use a device we call a blade (though it's not sharp, and doesn't cut) to move the patient's tongue out of view and move/lift other airway structures out of our view to directly visualize the trachea and vocal cords, while gently inserting an endotracheal tube that will ultimately get breaths into the patient's lungs.

We also must be extremely careful not to chip the patient's teeth, as this can easily happen with a novice performer.

This process requires a lot of practice, and anesthesia providers have more experience than any other specialty due to the frequency with which we perform the procedure.

I've intubated thousands of times, but never have I been scared for my life while doing it (that is about to change, and possibly forever). One cough from the patient (which commonly happens upon intubation) and I'm right in the line of fire. I would be exposed to a higher "viral load," or more virus particles.

A lot of places have intubation teams of people who wear extra PPE including a CAPR or PAPR system that has a hard hat like a construction worker might wear, and a full head and face enclosure with an electric component that purifies the air in it via hose for the best possible protection against airborne particles. They look like they are wearing hazmat suits, with head enclosures similar to what an astronaut might wear in space.

There is speculation that healthcare workers become sicker than the average healthy patient from being exposed to higher viral loads. Most of the time, medicine has research to confirm statements such as this, but with this virus being so new, there is so much information out there and some of it will be found to be inaccurate in the aftermath.

Everything is shared with good intentions, and nonetheless, intubation is one of the riskiest moments when caring for these patients. I'm also in a new hospital, and I don't know much of the equipment around me or where the supplies are located.

I take a deep breath.

Here we go.

CHAPTER 3

Wednesday, 8:30 a.m.

A respiratory therapist (RT) and an RN enter OR 14 to deliver my first patient. They help transfer her from a stretcher to the ICU bed and disappear back from where they came. Instantly, I'm struck with the current situation. The woman before me, in her mid-60s, is thrashing and trying to sit up in the bed, running a big risk of extubating (pulling out her breathing tube).

Phew, she's already intubated.

I always have my patients in a deep, proper level of sedation or anesthesia in the OR, and I know immediately that either this amount or type of medication is not working for her.

Her self-extubating would be an absolute disaster. When a patient is already intubated with a breathing tube and on a ventilator, all of their breaths are contained within a closed system of tubes, so the risk of transmitting the virus through the air is significantly lower than when a patient walks in through the ER or is simply wearing an oxygen mask.

Patients can't talk with an endotracheal tube in place, as it blocks their vocal cords. It is very stimulating and uncomfortable, making people feel as if they are breathing through a straw and maybe even suffocating if confused because their nose can't assist with getting air into their lungs.

Looking around, I see there are now just two ICU RNs in the room with me. There are no doctors in here, or orders on how to proceed.

The RNs are not familiar with the vents or monitors, but I am so we quickly hook everything up. We hook up standard EKG (heart rhythm) monitors, a blood pressure cuff and a pulse oximeter (oxygen monitor).

The patient is on two different continuous intravenous (IV) medications for sedation: Propofol and Fentanyl.

Each is on a pump, but neither is being administered at a sufficient level, resulting in her extreme restlessness, confusion or discomfort. She needs more sedation or her body will use too much precious oxygen while thrashing, and she could possibly hurt herself or self-extubate (accidentally remove her breathing tube), the latter of which could hurt us all.

OK, OK. Assess and respond.

Luckily with my anesthesia and sedation training, I am comfortable bolusing (giving more of the medication quickly) and then dealing with the effects.

The nurses were so thankful for my help as I worked her down to a level where she doesn't thrash any more, and I begin tweaking her ventilator settings because she is breathing too fast and in turn fighting the work the ventilator is trying to do.

The ventilator must coordinate with her efforts to make sure her breaths are large enough to oxygenate and ventilate her body as best as possible. She also needs IV medication to control her unstable and low blood pressure that I quickly start.

This means she will need closer blood pressure monitoring, so I start an arterial line that will continuously track her blood pressure with every heartbeat. It will also allow us to monitor her blood gases (labs) and decide on oxygen and ventilator changes from there.

This is an invasive, sterile procedure that requires skill and practice that RNs aren't trained to do, but yet another place where CRNAs are well equipped to help.

This is a necessary monitor when patients have unstable blood pressure as we don't have to wait for the standard non-invasive blood pressure cuff to take time to inflate and deflate to get a reading, not to mention that if blood pressure is low, these cuffs tend to be inaccurate or spend too much time pumping up and may never give a reading at all.

The RNs keep thanking me for my presence, but I barely hear them just now. The patient is not stable, but she's better than when she came in.

I'm still adjusting her IV medications for sedation and blood pressure, as well as making frequent changes to her ventilator. We've been in the room for almost an hour now, under all these layers of protective gear, and we are stifling hot.

It's also hard to talk from behind the barriers; we all sound very nasally and basically have to yell to be understood, adding to a situation that's already chaotic.

Everyone has to regularly repeat themselves, with countless, "Huh?" and "I can't hear you" exclamations only adding to the frustration.

I call out to the helpers in the hall and ask them to turn down the heat in the rooms; there are no thermostats in here. Almost all of the patients have fevers, so this move will help them, too.

There are OR staff members stationed in the hall to help grab needed equipment for us because once we don all the PPE, we would contaminate everything by walking out of the room.

The OR was emptied before it transitioned to an ICU so as to not contaminate the equipment that was in there, so we call out for a lot of supplies and someone slips open the door and drops it into a bin.

This is another thing that makes this OR assignment favorable compared to the ICU, step down units and other makeshift ICUs, where there aren't extra hands on deck.

There is a long rectangular window outside of every OR here, and we can see three or four masked faces staring in at us while we work, which is helpful but kind of weird at the same time to see. In a way, I feel like a caged zoo animal.

There are no more surgeries going on at this hospital except for C-sections and absolute life-saving emergencies. The rest have been shipped to neighboring hospitals that haven't been hit as hard by NOVA (for now — the other close hospitals will all be hit hard, but not quite *this* hard, within the week).

The OR staff made up of surgical technologists, circulating RNs and other ancillary help still need income too, so they are out in the hall to be our runners.

We frequently call out to them for supplies. Thankfully, they are eager to help, and they know where the equipment is.

We appreciate all the help we can get.

CHAPTER 4

Wednesday, 9:30 a.m.

In rolls our next patient to OR 14, with the same respiratory therapist as before. Our team of three works together like a well-oiled machine even though we first met a whole 60 minutes ago.

I make the ventilator transfer as quickly as possible, because any time we open or disconnect the circuit, the risk of transmitting the virus in the air is high. This woman, too, is fighting the ventilator. She requires soft wrist restraints to keep her from reaching her breathing tube and her sedation needs a lot of adjusting to make everyone safer.

I say a silent thank-you to the ER staff for doing the right thing and intubating her before the transfer.

Her situation is pretty similar to her new roommate's and although these circumstances were foreign to me an hour ago, I find myself settling down a bit to manage care.

My mind was frantic earlier with thoughts of the unknown (*I don't have time for your songs today, Elsa!*), but my medical training and experience are steadily winning this battle. I make a few mental notes of situations, supplies and surroundings in hopes they might come in handy down the road.

I find myself going back and forth between the two patients as the first woman still needs a lot of my attention, too.

A surgeon, who is now functioning as a NOVA ICU doctor, enters the room. The intensivists, other ICU doctors and pulmonologists (who specialize in respiratory health) are busy in the ICU with the other 60+ patients on vents.

This crisis has forced doctors to function outside of their normal capacity ... actually most staff, for that matter. We are desperate for all healthcare providers, and some schools even allowed medical students to graduate early in order to join the NOVA response.

I expected my new role, only because I read all about the harsh reality in Italy, where there are no more orthopedic doctors, trauma doctors, cardiologists, urologists, etc. to care for patients.

We are all living the same nightmare now and aren't fighting bones, car accidents or UTIs for the time being. We are all forced to care for the one and only monster problem called NOVA.

These doctors are required to think back to their medical school training programs, some which occurred decades ago. They are now trying to recall information that is irrelevant in their typical everyday roles; knowledge that now could potentially save a life or the alternative.

I feel bad for these physicians as they didn't sign up for this either. A lot of them aren't prepared.

I start my new patient's arterial line in her left radial (wrist) artery, same as I had with the last patient. I now have three pairs of gloves on, as this is a sterile procedure requiring special protection for the patients. I have never put on sterile gloves (most gloves are considered clean, not sterile) over top of gloves like this, and it's no easy task.

Donning sterile gloves entails a completely different process than applying regular gloves. One must be vigilant not to contaminate the sterile gloves with bare hands, or, in this case, the gloves I already have on.

The arterial line insertion goes quickly, smoothly and uneventfully. I am about to put on the sterile clear sticker to secure the arterial line when the surgeon instructs me to suture (sew) it in place.

I tell her these are great two-stage dressings made to hold the lines in place so they don't need to be stitched in (They are a bit of a newer advancement, and she's probably never seen them).

She responds that the line needs to be stitched, and I counter that I'm very familiar with these because I use them at another facility, but she doesn't let it go.

Instead, she opens a central line (a large neck IV that terminates near the heart to deliver fluids and medications) sterile kit that she is about to use, hands me the suture kit from inside of it and orders me to stitch the line.

I have lost the argument, but it's OK because I am very comfortable suturing these lines because I have to stitch them at one of the facilities where I regularly work that doesn't have these fancy two-stage dressings.

Except ... this is a much bigger needle than I'm used to, and I've never been in this environment. Nor have I been wearing so many pairs of gloves while doing it.

I begin the process, puncturing through her skin to secure the line, but somehow knick myself with the needle as it exits the other side. In that brief second, I feel a tiny bit of a sharp sensation on my left middle knuckle.

Inside, I am in a full panic, wondering if this is the moment I contract NOVA.

My patient's blood touched the needle before it poked me. I try to quickly finish suturing while staring at my knuckle and praying that I don't see my own blood come through the three pairs of gloves at the knick site.

My heart is racing, but time is standing still at the same time. I see a spot of blood start to form on my knuckle as it soaks through all three pairs of gloves.

Oh, NO.

The walls in the room begin to close in on me.

I want to run out screaming, rip off my gloves and wash up with soap NOW, but I can't do that. I have to finish securing the line or it can come out. This would leave my patient to bleed profusely from a large puncture in the middle of her artery, where blood pulsates straight from the heart.

I also can't rip off my PPE, as taking it off the proper, controlled way is the most critical moment to avoid contaminating myself. (Remember the 16-minute video?)

At this moment, I'm so grateful for last night's phone conversation about PPE, or I may have just now ripped it all off haphazardly. I have to start by carefully tearing off my gown… but are we supposed to save them? I know supplies are limited, but I don't know the supply situation here.

Come on and sew it already.

I finish the suturing, take off my sterile gloves, walk toward the door and rip off my gown, careful to fold it on itself to cover the contaminated spots while forming a ball.

Then I have to sanitize my gloves since they are now dirty from touching the gown. I walk into the hallway. Then I have to carefully remove my outer mask and face shield, not letting it touch my face as I pull it away. Then I sanitize my gloves again.

This is taking forever. Get it off get it off get it off. I need to scrub the finger NOW.

I envision a cartoon-looking virus with an evil laugh from a child's educational show starting to slowly take over my body. It doesn't help my panic.

Next I have to get my N95 respirator off, being careful not to touch the front portion as I know this has to be saved and rationed.

I put it in a paper bag with my name on it. I'm afraid to touch it again later but know I'll have to. My heart is still pounding as I wonder if this patient could actually be NOVA positive … and what about HIV or hepatitis?

These patients came to me directly from the ER, so while testing for NOVA has been done, it still takes days for the results to come back. We are treating everyone as if they have it, but it's not confirmed at this time. Their clinical presentation suggests they are, in fact, NOVA positive.

These are moments you don't consider when you decide you want to be a CRNA. You don't think about putting your physical well-being at risk.

I want so badly to scrub the hand, but I still have to sanitize my gloves and meticulously remove both pairs. Finally, my hands are bare. I stand at the scrub sink, washing my knuckle and staring at the small skin abrasion. It has broken my skin … exactly what I prayed wouldn't happen.

Am I supposed to try to squeeze some blood out of the puncture site?

Is this the moment that will change my life forever? I don't know anyone here. I don't know where the Employee Health Department even is.

A nurse comes up to me and can see I'm shaken. I calmly tell her that I have a needlestick injury. All five people around me in the hall gasp. *Oh, no.*

And their looks say it all.

CHAPTER 5

Wednesday, 10:45 a.m.

A nurse helps me to get the proper employee incident form filled out and start the process of drawing the source patient's blood. We have to test the patient for HIV and hepatitis to determine if I will need to be treated for those conditions. Whoever's drawing her blood is in luck: The same line that caused my injury can be used to quickly draw blood and requires no skill or additional needle poke to do so.

Someone hands me a Band-Aid which I eventually put on the pinpoint-sized puncture after what feels like nine minutes of scrubbing a knuckle with so much soap, as if I have some control of the final effect this may have on me.

Someone else gets my attention and points out a window. The Employee Health Department — where I'll need to go to be seen by a doctor and an RN who take care of health problems encountered by employees — is just through those two parking lots over there and past the parking garage if you walk down through the…

All I can hear is the teacher's voice from Charlie Brown.

Wah wah wah wah wah wah wah wah wah.

My world is spinning. From what I can gather, the Employee Health Department is basically in a different area code and I'm never going to find it.

I put on a new basic mask and begin my trek with a patient sticker to identify the elderly woman. Of course, I'm already lost by the time I get downstairs. You know, the exact place I thought I was told I could exit the building.

The hospital seems completely dead two floors below the OR. It is eerie, and looks a little too much to me like the set of a horror movie. Maybe one with a war scene, or something where the apocalypse has begun.

The lights above my head are old, and appear to buzz and flicker. I'm in an area where typically many people walk around from maintenance, housekeeping, linen staff — anyone — and I can't find a single one to ask where I am or where I'm going.

Is this the never-ending hallway, too? It feels about a mile long.

I even yell "Hello?" down the hall. It echoes back with no reply.

Finally after walking a bit, I see a housekeeper in a mask and he directs me back upstairs. In a wonderful twist of fate, I run into the director on my journey and he calls a shuttle to take me to Employee Health.

As instructed, I start a claim with the worker's compensation team on the phone while awaiting a shuttle. The hospital needs to know about this in case treatment is necessary: This is a standard procedure.

I feel like I'm floating above myself, watching this scene unfold. As with many things I'll face during my two days in Detroit, this situation feels completely surreal.

I am in shock, which makes me much calmer than reason tells me I should be. I feel like my feet are made of stone. Time is moving so slowly and everything seems a little blurry.

I must have it (the virus) now. ... But I will be fine. Right? My immune system will beat this. I will not be another one of these poor people on a ventilator. This just can't be what God has in store for me.

I pray to God all the while. I pray that my family's prayers for protection are working, I pray this woman is HIV and hepatitis negative ... the list is endless.

The shuttle is here. I'm thankful it's a mild, sunny day as I don't have a coat, just my scrubs and — remember, it's March in Michigan. The driver is wearing her N95 mask and the two seats closest her are blocked off according to the social distancing rules that urge everyone to keep 6 feet apart.

I'm the only passenger. There is nothing normal about what NOVA has done to the world, and with each little tidbit I observe, my entire experience grows more and more surreal. Even bus drivers are at risk: A young Detroit busdriver would later die of COVD-19 after posting on social media about passengers coughing on his bus. Tragic.

Three minutes later, I arrive at a new building and have to pass through an entrance that's guarded by security, just like I did at the start of the day.

"Up the elevator to the end of the hall," the guard directs. I find the office and sign in like patients do.

I'm now a patient. I can't believe I'm sitting here in this situation. I came all this way as a provider to help patients, now I AM one.

I turn on my phone for the first time since my arrival and find a multitude of texts from coworkers in my hometown. I have told very few people I was coming here as it all happened so fast, but it seems like it was breaking news on television or even an amber alert on the cell phone with the overwhelming amount of texts and questions coming through.

People are asking if I was actually there helping. The way it sounds, it's almost as if "there" means Mars or some place no man had gone before. This isn't helping my growing concern about the current situation.

Unbeknownst to me, another situation is already brewing. All too soon, I will be treated with a negative stigma because I answered this call to help. I never could have fathomed that offering my services where they were needed most would lead to me being ostracized by my work family back home.

But right now, I really just want to research my needlestick injury and am distracted by the text messages. I use Google to search on my phone as I wait to be called in a feverish attempt to learn if NOVA can be transmitted by a needle stick injury via blood.

It's not as easy to find as I hope — this is a new disease and there just isn't enough research yet — but it turns out that it *shouldn't* be able to be transmitted that way, just via airborne particles that are inhaled or via direct contact with mucus membranes.

…but does anyone really know this yet? HIV is a virus and it can be transmitted by blood. Why would this be different?

My gut tells me it can absolutely be transmitted that way, based off of zero research.

Everything is so new with this novel virus. I am slightly comforted by my findings, now all that's left to worry about is whether I've contracted HIV and/or hepatitis…gee, aren't I lucky.

A masked nurse checks me in and somehow my blood pressure and heart rate are normal. I allow myself a minute to be impressed, silently congratulating my physical self for holding the status quo while my mind continues to race. I turn my head away to take my own oral temperature as I have to remove my mask and want to protect the nurse. It's 97.7 degrees.

Normal for me considering all the excitement and walking.

When the doctor, also masked, comes in, I let him know I'm a non-converter to the hepatitis vaccines, which basically means that I won't ever be protected by them.

When I first became an RN, I had to go through a process of about nine pokes to learn this: A vaccine followed by two boosters, then a lab draw to see that there were no antibodies, then another booster, etc., all to hear I have no sure failsafe against hepatitis.

It's a pretty rare thing, and the doctor sarcastically says I'm part of the "lucky" 1 percent ... well I don't feel so lucky, especially right now. He says if the source patient *does* have hepatitis, I'll have to start the treatment protocol right away tomorrow.

I'm over 100 miles from home and will not be coming back tomorrow. He explains we won't know the hepatitis results until the next day as this lab test is done at another facility, and that I could get the treatment in my hometown, but they would coordinate it.

"The HIV results should be back by now," he says.

It's been almost an hour since I left the OR. He leaves to check the lab result system and quickly comes back to me with more annoying news.

"The lab never received a specimen from that patient," he says in a sympathetic tone.

"Hmmmph!" I say, shaking my head in disbelief.

Of course they didn't. This day is going so well.

I text the director and ask him to please have the patient's nurse get the proper specimens to the lab stat (ASAP), and he is happy to help. I later found out that a nurse had immediately drawn the source patient's blood and accidentally put it in the wrong type of specimen tube so it had to be discarded.

This got lost in the communication lines somewhere and another sample had not been drawn until my call.

In the meantime, the doctor wants me to have a hepatitis booster shot anyway, just in case, and get blood work drawn to see if the labs reveal any antibodies since there is no record of my non-converter status, just my word. I'm fine with that; I'll take any small chance of protection I can get.

They tell me to head to the lab on the first floor, so down the elevator I go. When I arrive I find the lab is closed because they don't want people coming in for labs in this location amidst the NOVA crisis.

Perfect, ugh. Now *where do I go?*

I imagine another long, eerie trek through an unfamiliar hospital in search of a lab.

I return to Employee Health and beg the nurse to draw my blood. She is very busy and not used to working in that department, but thankfully does it anyway. I'm eventually headed back to the hospital on another solo shuttle ride with a different masked driver.

The director is very comforting and helpful as I eat lunch in his office. He asks what I would like to do: I've been through a whole lot and it's still only 2:30 p.m. I tell him that I'll stay until 7 p.m. — the end of my 12-hour shift — since I already drove all this way. It would almost feel like a complete waste of my time and skills to leave now.

Can it really get worse anyway?

I've already gotten poked by a suspected NOVA patient's contaminated needle, and I'm going to finish my commitment.

"Great," he says, "we're starting a new NOVA ICU upstairs."

First, I answer a phone call with great news that the source patient in OR 14 doesn't have HIV. Huge relief.

Now just NOVA and hepatitis to worry about ... no big deal, right?

Upstairs, we go to a unit meant to start IVs, and prep and recover patients from outpatient procedures. Once he shows me the new location, the director wishes me luck and heads back to his office. There are approximately 20 rooms around the nurses' stations, and the rooms have clear glass doors.

I check out the supply room and am so comforted by the plentiful amount of gowns, gloves, face shields, N95s and sanitizers. I had heard from all over the news how horrible it is that healthcare workers are at risk because of a lack of PPE, and the amount I see here is a beautiful thing.

I can only hope it lasts for the duration of the crisis. I can already tell it's going to be a marathon, not a sprint.

I see a few nurses sitting around the station, but no patients yet. I see anesthesia machines (now intended to be utilized as ventilators as in the OR) in about six of the rooms and realize they are just making ICUs wherever there is space.

I talk to the nurses to get their backgrounds. One of them works in an alcohol outpatient rehab center where she doesn't have physical contact with patients, one is an ICU nurse, a couple are endoscopy nurses who usually work in the rooms where colonoscopies and the like are performed, and one is a Nurse Practitioner (NP) who works in an outpatient clinic and has some previous ICU experience.

The ICU nurse is experienced with vented patients, but the others are not trained for these situations and are scared.

Remember, on a pre-NOVA-crisis day, there is a nursing shortage in the nation. This pandemic has made a huge increased need for nurses on top of that. No hospital can prepare for a 10-fold increased need for ICU nurses overnight. They have been calling for anyone in nursing to come out of retirement; any help is taken. Nurses from all over the nation are here to help.

I am glad to have willing RNs and help there. We are all so far out of our comfort zones, and I admire their bravery for showing up. Some are there by their own accord.

The hospital has done a great job getting people there at a time when most want to just stay home. In fact, the state is under "Stay At Home" orders and people are not supposed to leave unless absolutely essential.

If what we're doing here isn't the definition of "essential," I don't know what is.

The people around me dove in head-first to help, not knowing what they might encounter. They showed so much courage. At the same time, they won't know certain things that I request of them.

Not only am I on a different floor than before, but there are not nearly as many staff members to run for help with supplies. I'm also used to the equipment I need being footsteps away. It is now on another floor, and no one here will know what I'm referring to if I ask for it.

Problem-solving time. I ask for a bin because I need to return to the anesthesia supply area and gather supplies. I find another CRNA to help.

I rack my brain to think of everything I used in my first two admissions. Fluids, IVs, arterial line kits, EKG stickers ... the list goes on and on, and the bin starts to overflow before we know it.

When we return, I begin to realize how much smaller these rooms are than the ORs and try to envision a patient on a stretcher, the ICU bed, our large anesthesia machines and all of the other equipment that needs to be rearranged for logistics. Right after making some space, the first patient to our newest NOVA ICU rolls in. I quickly step aside to properly don the same overwhelming amount of PPE that I did this morning.

Here we go again.

CHAPTER 6

Wednesday, 4:45 p.m.

The respiratory therapist (RT) who is wheeling the patient in is the same one from this morning, and I can read the exhaustion on his face despite the bottom half of his face being covered by a mask. The RTs are transporting these patients all over the hospital. They are also in charge of the ventilators for all of the patients in the hospital who aren't using the anesthesia machines, and right now, they are working significantly beyond their normal capacity.

These professionals are also probably present with every intubation that the CRNAs or ER physicians perform, and are at high risk every minute of this war. I thank him for what he is doing.

Wait.

Something is very different with this patient. This man with a breathing tube on the vent is *wide awake*.

No. I'm not sure how to handle this. Maybe I should "slam" him to sleep as soon as I can? I KNOW I can keep him safe once he's asleep!

Does he even have sedation started? I see he has a few IV pumps.

This is so unusual.

The patient — who's around 60 years old — is intubated but sitting straight up on the stretcher, looking at us and cooperative. He almost looks as if he could smile and wave as he rolls in.

He is not fighting, but he is not restrained either. The latter of this means he is at risk of pulling out the endotracheal tube which would lead to a whole slew of consequences.

Because I typically work in surgery and in the business of giving anesthesia or sedation, I am not used to patients being awake and intubated, much less trying to communicate with them while they're like this.

I realize that the RT and RN have been with him for far longer than I have (some patients have been in the ER for more than four hours while awaiting a ventilator, an ICU room and/or staff to be freed up), and it's obviously been working for them.

I've also never talked to patients while I'm wearing the complete hazmat suit of PPE, although I'm assuming they do in emergency rooms all the time these days. It's a far departure from my long, storied experience — I've admitted all of two patients in this role so far — but it's the hand I've been dealt.

As I'm processing this new experience in my head, the large African American man in front of me gingerly moves himself from his cart to his new ICU bed in Room 12 as I support the tubing from his ventilator.

This is something I have never seen in my 20 years in healthcare. I realize this poor man has to be absolutely petrified. I tell him my name as I hook him up to the ventilator. Now, it's just me and the ICU nurse with him.

I squeeze his hand in my gloved hand in a silent gesture of comfort while assuring him that I will help him breathe.

Then we hook him up to the monitors and begin to assess what we have to work with. I quickly get to work, taking in how many IVs he has and how poorly he is oxygenating. I'm also tweaking the ventilator modes and oxygen settings to work with his 35 breaths per minute (I'm seeing a pattern start to develop in these NOVA patients).

A normal respiratory rate is less than 20 breaths per minute, and I'm not surprised to see this is how they initially manifest themselves. Now to assess if I can trust this fully conscious man.

Deep breath.

I position myself directly in front of him and stare into his eyes through my face shield. In my most serious mom voice, I tell him, "I *need*. To be *able*. To *trust you*." I hope my eyes are communicating just how serious this is. "You CANNOT touch that breathing tube. Nod your head 'yes' if you understand."

My mom voice doesn't tend to hold much weight for my own 4-year-old son at home, and I'm hoping it works better tonight on this adult stranger, a man decades my senior.

The man nods.

"If you touch the tube, we will have to restrain you. If you dislodge that tube, you could die really quickly, and you will put us (I motion to the RN) at risk. Do you understand?"

He nods again.

"Now. Are you feeling like it's getting harder to breathe and that you need more help? Are you getting tired?"

He shakes his head. "No."

"OK. Are you feeling scared or anxious? Nervous? I can sedate you and give you medicine to help you. Do you want me to give you medicine for that now?"

He shakes his head "No" again.

"I am going to be here with you, and we are monitoring you."

I realize that in order to place the arterial line (one of the next steps for vented patients), I will need to use local anesthetic to numb him since he is wide awake. I call out to a helper in the hallway to find me some Lidocaine, a small needle and syringe to numb him, as well as sterile gloves in my size …

Shoot! I forgot to grab those on my trip downstairs for supplies.

What else did I forget?

As I wait for that equipment, I realize this man is also burning up and sweating. I ask for cool washcloths to comfort him, and pillows to place behind his knees. He is a very tall man and his feet are right up against the hard footboard, so I want to pad that area too.

If he is going to be awake, I want to make him as comfortable as possible for as long as possible. This is a move of compassion, but also it's important to keep his blood pressure normal and to conserve the sedation, since rumor is that the hospital is running out of it.

This is one of the most troublesome things I have heard all day. No sedation will be an absolute nightmare!

He is coughing a lot and needs to be suctioned. This is uncomfortable to have done, but I am thankful that the RT in the ER had the patient all set with inline suction right on the end of the breathing tube.

This saves us from another chance of exposure if we had to hook this up ourselves, or from having to go the old school route in which we disconnect the circuit and send an exposed catheter through the open end of the breathing tube, deep into the lungs.

This man is familiar with the suction process, since he's been on the ventilator and awake for more than an hour. I ask if he's ready and when he confirms, I send the sterile tube down into his lungs and press the button to suction the mucus as I withdraw the suction catheter.

He's visibly uncomfortable and coughing as aggressively as one can, but indicates I should do one more pass.

He seems better now, but he has saliva and mucus dripping from his mouth as well. I suction that and wipe him with the washcloths. I'm trying to treat this terrified man with as much dignity and kindness as possible.

I can't imagine how scared he is. I know how scared *I* am, and take a minute to marvel at how brave this man is. I feel a connection to him.

My gloves arrive for the arterial line, so I start sterilely prepping his wrist and securing it in an extended position. I tell him I will numb him, but when he sees the needle, his eyes grow cartoonishly large. I grab his hand and tell him he can do this.

"The needle doesn't go in very far at all — just barely under the surface of the skin — and will only feel like a bee sting for a few seconds as the Lidocaine is injected. It won't be that bad; I know you can take it."

He nods his head in silent understanding and gently turns his head away so he can't see what I'm about to do.

I quickly numb the area with more than enough Lidocaine. He should just feel pressure for the duration, and I assure him the worst is over. The procedure goes very quickly and smoothly, and I take a minute to thank God for that. These lines can be tricky as they are done solely by feel because you can't visualize an artery through the skin with your eyes.

I use the nice two-stage dressing to secure it, God knows after this morning that I do not want to suture anything else today. There's a risk any time we use needles.

I get the man settled in, constantly assessing how he is doing mentally and assuring him I can help him relax at any moment. I give him a call light to summon us if he needs something. It is quite unorthodox to give an intubated patient a call light. In general, these types of patients are restrained, sedated and unable to tell anyone their needs, for safety precautions.

This man is a ticking time bomb though, and I know his peace won't last … he will eventually need sedation. His lungs will get worse, and we will have to minimize his oxygen consumption with sedation.

He will also slowly become confused as the disease takes its course.

But for now we will honor his wishes and reassess frequently. I tell him we will be monitoring him from the desk, and that he is not alone, but remind him that we can't just run in to help.

"So when you push the light, look for us from the glass door as we have to take three or four minutes to put on our masks and gowns before we enter the room, so try to have patience with us. We are here with you, I promise."

We realize there are TVs in these rooms connected to the walls, as they are typically used as waiting areas, and swivel one from the corner to a position where he can see it.

My mind is just blown from the events of the day already. I can't believe my eyes as I look in on this large man, who's sitting up in bed, watching TV with cool cloths on his head, on a ventilator!

I wonder what TV show he is watching right now? Will it be the last one he ever sees?

My head spins with all that's gone on. I'm wondering at what moment is this going to take a serious turn for the worse. I *know* he will get worse.

They all do once they're on a ventilator.

I don't want *anyone* to get worse, but I feel a closer connection to this man and really don't want to see him decline.

I take off all of my PPE just in time to see another patient rolling in.

CHAPTER 7

Wednesday, 6 p.m.

My newest patient is a woman in her mid-70s who presents in a similar fashion to the first two OR patients: She's fighting the ventilator and a risk of self extubation. She undergoes the same admission process, but this time enters with an endoscopy nurse who, for obvious reasons, isn't as prepared for this new role as an ICU nurse.

First, I get her sedated properly. Next, I prepare the patient for her arterial line and ask the RN to start a second IV as these patients are going to need that at the very least.

She tells me she doesn't feel comfortable starting IVs. I feel myself get slightly frustrated internally by her response as at a minimum, every RN has had to start IVs in school, but then almost immediately start to feel sympathetic toward these nurses. They aren't prepared for this, and it's not their fault. They are probably wonderful endoscopy nurses — they may be the best in their field — but this crisis has pushed everyone so far beyond their comfort zone and skill levels that it's just crazy.

How hard would it be for them without a CRNA or confident advanced practice provider or physician with them? They don't typically need to know how to care for ICU patients, and that includes ventilators, IV sedating medications or blood pressure medications.

Thankfully, I have yet to feel that something needed to be done that I couldn't handle at this point; it's just that I don't have the supplies, meds or resources on hand like I usually do.

I'm also restricted to stay in the room and can't just zip out to grab things as the gowns and my PPE would contaminate the area. We also have yet to see one physician since this new unit opened.

They are all extremely busy in other areas of the hospital and probably don't even know about this new unit, as their census list is unlike anything they've ever experienced.

Census lists are lists for physicians and advanced practice nurses that tell them which patients are "theirs" and who needs to be rounded on (seen by them), as not every patient is seen by every provider normally.

In this current situation, the physicians wouldn't even know what this new unit was called if it did show up on their list, as there has never been an inpatient assigned to these beds in this hospital before right now.

I'm having trouble with one of the monitor cables when a CRNA that I haven't yet met walks in and tells me he has been assigned to the actual ICU for the past 12 hours. He is extremely helpful and confident. I am in my full suit of PPE and he walks into my patient's room with none of that — not even a basic mask, let alone an N95.

Huh? Is this all a dream after all?

I inquire about that, and he proceeds to nonchalantly tell me that the general consensus is that "this place is crawling with NOVA and all of us probably already have it."

He's acting like it's no big deal at all. He has been there all week, and I imagine he started as vigilant as I am with the PPE, but over time became desensitized and sick of it?

I wonder how many other people have done the same. I can't imagine letting myself get to that point, but I certainly envy the carefree mentality that is the antithesis of mine. I have to make every effort to not bring this home to my husband and children, and I have no clue what this guy's life situation is like, but it's all a personal choice.

I want to keep my exposure and viral load as low as possible for as long as possible.

A third patient comes rolling into this new unit. Another CRNA and an endoscopy RN admit a man in his late 50s, which makes three vented patients in the new unit.

The ER staff must have been so happy to transfer out three critical patients in a fairly short amount of time.

You've survived the day. It's almost time to leave. There's a light at the end of this dark tunnel. I gain a little pep in my step thinking about this.

My shift ends around 7 p.m. Just then, I see a text on my phone —I turned it on when I had my two hour excursion to Employee Health earlier— asking me to stay until 11 p.m.

Oof. I want to go home so badly, but I also know how badly I'm needed here. ... Will I ever feel like I can leave though?

I agree to meet in the middle and stay until 9ish because I have a two-hour drive home still ahead of me tonight and I'm exhausted.

I huddle up all the new nurses because it's shift change and several doe-eyed young RNs have reported for duty. These nurses are ICU nurses at another facility who came to answer the call for help but had no clue what they were in for either. Like me, they have probably never been in this hospital and don't *have* to be here, either. More heroes on the list of thousands.

I am keeping an eye on the medications that sedate these patients and ask the nurses to order more from the pharmacy. They aren't used to keeping patients sedated, and I'm not used to having to call the pharmacy for drugs as in a normal situation, I have all of my anesthesia drugs right by me and can get them instantly.

We can't wait for a medication to run out; we have to remain vigilant. If we don't prepare, the patients will wake up, and that leads to a whole group of problems. The pharmacists need time to process the orders and get them sent through the tube systems (kind of like the drive-thru at the bank) to the proper unit, and as long as I'm on the clock, I want things to move forward as smoothly as possible given the circumstances.

After speaking with the pharmacy, they report back that the hospital is out of Versed, and set to run out of Propofol and Fentanyl in the next few hours.

These are the three most common IV drugs used to keep a patient calm and sedated while vented.

I have a horrible sinking feeling growing in my stomach. Without sedation, these patients are going to be unmanageable. I might not be here at that point, but how will those nurses left behind manage?

I picture these poor nurses alone with thrashing patients who are requiring much more oxygen because they're agitated.

They might have to physically hold these confused patients down so they don't hurt themselves.

I can't think of a worse position for a nurse to be in: having no control over a patient and no one to quickly replace the breathing tube if the patient self extubates.

I'm scared for them. We have to ration these drugs. I start to decrease everyone's sedation to the lowest amount possible to just keep them from moving too much (there is some wiggle room, pardon the pun, as they don't have to be paralyzed to be safe). I'm grateful that my guy in spot 12 is awake and not medicated (yet), because he would be going through huge amounts of sedation due to his age and stature.

With sedation it's almost all or nothing because when you give them "just a little," you never know the point at which they are too confused to be trusted and all you-know-what can break loose. Once he starts with sedation, he's going to need a lot from that moment on.

I'm saddened to realize that my three patients here are such a tiny piece of the big picture.

This medication rationing will likely be an unnoticed drop in the bucket system-wide, but still, I can only control my piece.

I ask them to call the pharmacy now and get every sedation option, whether oral or IV. I tell them they'll need a plan, and that if they are forced to use oral meds, they'll need to put in oral gastric tubes (¼-inch plastic tubes that go in the patient's mouth and are advanced into the stomach, a usually simple task) ASAP and get those meds started.

Our guy in spot 12 will not tolerate that tube placement while awake.

Although the placement of the tube is simple, the patient is quite stimulated and uncomfortable. Unlike IV medications, oral meds take time to work and are going to be much weaker in their action.

They need to be administered long before they're truly needed in order to be effective.

We peer through the glass doors as I start to give the new troops a crash course in anesthesia machine ventilators from the door. "See that button there, that does this, this means this," and "In case of emergency, push this; scroll here." They are feverishly nodding and taking notes, eyes bugging out.

ICU nurses are used to having a respiratory therapist readily available to manage the ventilators, but these are anesthesia machines and respiratory therapists wouldn't be familiar with them even if they were available ... which they aren't.

I don't know what the overnight situation is for CRNA resources as I am leaving at 9 p.m., and the other CRNA who arrived to this unit later leaves at 11.

We can't stay forever.

These nurses are so brave and I'm so honored to share the RN in my title of CRNA with them. A house nurse supervisor (who covers the entire hospital) comes walking through the department with someone who I think is the Chief Nursing Officer and an administrative physician right before 9 p.m.

They are calling me an "angel" and are thanking me from the bottom of their hearts for my services today, knowing that I traveled more than a hundred miles to help.

I appreciate their words and gratitude, but it all rings hollow right now. I don't feel good about myself, or *anything* for that matter.

The situation is exactly as I read it was in Italy, and there are no positive things happening in the hospital from the little I have seen. No staff discussing gossip, talking about their home lives ... nothing. Is there even anything else to even talk about in the world?

Sports were canceled and the news has nothing but NOVA coverage 24/7. The mood is so serious and somber, and the halls are empty and it's just ... *eerie.*

While my shift is winding down, I ask the house supervisor some questions about the status of the hospital since I'm completely unfamiliar with it. She tells me that the hospital normally has 36 ICU beds.

To me, that means they're probably used to having 28 vents at a time (on a busy day), as a portion of ICU patients are critical but not on vents. At that moment there are 65 vented patients in-house!

They have never needed so many, as is the case for all the hardest-hit areas in the U.S. right now.

This is where all the currently underused anesthesia machines came into play. I know of places pulling old "antique" ventilators out of their basements and having the biomedical engineers repair them to function again.

A "dinosaur" ventilator is better than no ventilator. Italy would've loved to have more dinosaur ventilators.

The hospital has converted the step-down unit (a floor normally reserved for patients who are not quite sick enough to need ICU care, but their condition is still guarded) into a full-fledged vented ICU.

These rooms have regular wood opaque doors and no windows. Most ICU rooms have glass doors so the patients can be seen at all times from the nurses station.

You can't look in on these patients without opening the doors and letting the contaminated air flow freely. So doors are shut and every room is occupied by a vented patient.

This also means that a lot of these nurses aren't used to caring for vented patients.

Now the vented units include the standard ICU, the step-down unit, the Post Anesthesia Care Unit or PACU (meant for an hour of post-surgery recovery), ORs and now this outpatient unit, plus an emergency room that is backed up as people wait for rooms with vents and staff.

Some ER patients are on transport ventilators (meant for very short use) for hours.

I have only seen a tiny piece of this nightmare, and it is chilling.

There's a bright side, though: The nursing supervisor tells me she hopes to have four patients taken off their vents tonight and raises her arms to cheer.

She is so happy, as if it is her own family member recovering. From what I'm told, the NOVA surge in this hospital started late the previous Saturday and into Sunday morning, so these are among the first patients to be extubated, or get better.

They were vented for five days, which is on the very short end from what I will later put together.

It's a small victory, and a step in the right direction. At the same time, I know that means four more patients will need those vents, and that's a best-case scenario.

Those extubated patients would have to sustain their breathing without the vent, which is far from a guarantee. None of the patients I have admitted today will be confirmed NOVA positive for at least another day as they were direct ER admits to me and those tests take time (still anywhere from three to five days at this stage of the game).

Everyone assumes they are all positive with the overwhelming influx of patients with respiratory distress and pneumonia, however.

There is also the false negative factor to consider. A high percentage (upward of 30 percent) of negative test results are actually positive upon retesting, another unsettling fact. This means we can never truly let our guard down, even upon reading a negative test result.

As I prepare to leave, I think back to the start of this shift. It seems days ago now that I walked through the doors to meet this monster head-on. So much has happened in the past 14 hours that it seems like an alternate reality.

CHAPTER 8

Wednesday, 9:25 p.m.

Finally, I get to leave, but not before I spend a solid three minutes using sterilizing wipes and clean gloves to disinfect my phone that had been protected in a bag anyway, and my name badge that I can't throw away. The manager has left me some soap, and I head to the locker room shower, forming a checklist in my head about which things I can touch after I've showered without causing contamination.

This virus is terrifying. I have never wanted to shower more in my life.

There are some garbage bags nearby, so I grab one and cram my underwear, socks and bra inside. I reorganize my clean clothes three times while near the shower to make sure they don't touch anything I've already touched.

And then, I scrub my body starting with my neck that was always exposed and every single surface of my body with the cheap bar of hospital soap.

My sensitive skin is going to be bothered by this soap for a while, but that's the least of my worries at this point.

I scrub furiously, not stopping until the entire bar of soap has disappeared. My long hair is going to be a ratty mess after washing it with a bar of hospital soap since I don't have shampoo or a comb to use.

Then, I dry off and carefully put on my street clothes, mindful not to touch anything but the clean clothes.

Oops.

I didn't think this part through. I forgot to bring clean underwear and socks into the hospital. I get to put on my 15-year-old pair of jeans and go commando ... yikes, chafing!

Levitation would come in so handy right now! Or flying, or anything where I don't have to touch anything!

I tiptoe around the shower, certain I look ridiculous.

I grab my garbage bag and leave the locker room. I just have to get out of the building now.

Don't touch anything ... you're finally clean.

I clumsily push the elevator button with the elbow of my old coat and arrive at the main floor. I can see the exit!

One problem: They have closed the main entrance to the hospital since it is now almost 10 p.m. and they don't have the manpower to screen people at entrances. There is a sign on the wall that directs me to the ER, my only exit.

Gulp.

I look around frantically to see if there are any other exits. I don't see any. I'm even prepared to run through one of those doors that says "No Exit, Alarm Will Sound."

The ER is the last place on earth I want to be right now. That's where all the sick people come in without barriers over their mouths.

There could be 50 contagious people in there. But I don't have a choice, so I head down the hall, giving myself a pep talk as I go.

You're almost there. This is almost over. You can do this.

I need to be buzzed into the ER since it is locked (as are many ERs, for safety reasons) and my badge doesn't work as a key in this facility.

It's dimly lit inside as I enter the waiting room, and all around me are people wearing masks who are not employees. These are potential patients and their rides.

I start to jog. I make awkward progress, since I have on sneakers and no socks, which feels terrible. The space is so small and there are so many people in here!

Get me out of here. How did I get here?

Panic bubbles up inside me. I draw a deep breath, like I'm about to dive to the bottom of the ocean, and begin to sprint.

I am running through an Emergency Room in Detroit with wet hair and the hood up on my old coat. I've got no underwear on, and am carrying a garbage bag of my belongings that swings awkwardly beside me as I dodge people in masks while trying not to breathe.

I put my arm up to my face to attempt to cover my mouth and nose.

I was actually starring in a horror movie without the camera. I wanted to scream and cry at the same time. I finally find the exit and continue sprinting to my car like I'm being chased by a villain.

More than anything in the world, I want to be home right now, but I have a long, dark and lonely commute ahead of me.

Once I get on the road, I call my husband to tell him I'm alive and that I won't be home until after 11:30 p.m. I pass a few liquor stores, Coney Islands and run-down hotels with bright flashing Vegas-like lights before I get to the highway.

I pass the time on the ride talking to a friend on the phone while driving on an empty I-75 at 80 mph. I need to decompress to a knowledgeable good friend and nurse who I can safely cry to as any exhausted mom does. The roads are clear, and I floor it.

I realize a little while later that I am famished and pull off at an exit where there are plenty of options for fast food ... except when I get there I see they have all already closed for the night.

I forgot that this is the apocalypse, so even Taco Bell closes at 9 p.m. No "Fourth Meal" during a pandemic.

Back on the highway, I eventually see a 24-hour fast food sign and am just still in disbelief of what is happening in my world due to the crazy animal practices in Asia. I mean, even Taco Bell closed at nine, what a telling sign of the times.

I feel a huge sense of relief and comfort, the food beginning to settle in my stomach, as I see the "Ohio Welcomes You" sign just ahead.

When I arrive home well after 11 p.m., I'm relieved to pull in the driveway but my day isn't over yet. I strip completely naked in the garage.

My clothes will stay in that garbage bag in the garage for two weeks before I'm brave enough to dump them into a washing machine full of scalding hot water.

I run through the house in my birthday suit, yelling "Hello!" over my shoulder to my bewildered husband on the couch as I streak toward the sanctity of our bathroom.

He's used to this no-contact-until-I'm-out-of-the-shower routine as I have been following it for the last few weeks anyway, but I have never been completely nude or running this fast. The Band-Aid from the hepatitis booster shot on my left shoulder and the bandage wrap from the lab draw on my left inner elbow almost glow in the dark on my naked body, and my husband comments on them.

I tell him we'll talk soon. I need to shower before anything else.

We need to start turning the heat on higher before I come home if I'm going to regularly streak through the house.

After I emerge, clean and pink from another round of frantic scrubbing, I begin to break down the past 24 hours for my husband.

I plop down on the couch and don't move a muscle besides my mouth. His mind is blown as I tell him the harsh reality of NOVA.

I am physically exhausted but still too wired to sleep. My head just keeps replaying the day on repeat. I keep seeing the awake intubated man and my punctured needlestick injury on my knuckle over and over.

This makes two nights in a row of anxious insomnia. I hate thinking about how I have been the last person to ever speak to people before they die, and that today, that may have happened again.

I think back on my career and certain emergencies where that has happened previously, and mentally prepare myself that this may happen often in the ensuing months.

It just makes me realize that it's so important to convey loving kindness and comfort to these people in their unknowing final moments.

Please, brain. I need some rest.

CHAPTER 9

Thursday, 5:45 a.m.

My day off starts way too early as my mind is too active to sleep, even though I'm in desperate need of rest. The whole day I think about my family. Should I be living somewhere else for a while? Some people quarantine themselves in campers or hotels. Chances are it's too late though; I've probably already infected the house.

My gut and prayer is that we were all exposed very early from a couple of airplane rides and a trip to Disney World last week. There, the kids learned that their mom would punish them worse than they have ever seen if caught picking their noses.

They also became appropriately aware of using all hand sanitizers and undergoing longer, more frequent hand-washing while singing songs to know how long to wash.

"Row, row, row your boat, gently down your knees," my cute 4-year-old would start singing as he washed.

Some good is going to come of this crisis. #SilverLinings

But we were still on an airplane, and there's a chance we had already built some immunity. One thing that provided me with comfort was that I had seen zero deaths of children under 10 years old in the entire world at that point, and almost no cases of them even getting noticeably sick.

They still carry the virus and can likely transmit it to others, but they won't suffer for my choices.

I worry about my husband and myself of course, but have such a strong faith in God and trust in his plan for our lives and take comfort in our healthy histories.

Prayer and prudence is the motto our church adopted, and I have been prudent with all that I could control with sanitizing, and I have been vigilant in prayer.

How would I even know when it's safe to come home if I lived elsewhere? It's not like I'd get a letter telling me I had the virus and am safe now. That could go on for months. I would lose my mind.

I'm so thankful my husband doesn't show his concerns or make me feel guilty in any way. Quite the opposite: He calls me a hero and hugs me tightly, showering me with love and support.

I am dealing with some Post Traumatic Stress Disorder-like symptoms that I have never experienced, and really now have an inkling of relatable empathy for veterans or others who suffer.

I'm not in any way trying to compare what veterans saw and what I did, I just mean that I now have an acute understanding that PTSD is all-consuming at times.

The haunting dreams are beyond awful. I am in need of support from friends and family more than ever, except I couldn't have contact with them due to the strict social distancing guidelines.

Still, I am very thankful I can hug my amazing family in the comfort of our home. My parents and siblings text often to check in on me as well.

I also have a handful of very supportive friends that reach out to check on me too, and I cry with each text of support and care. Between the lack of sleep and what I had seen, my emotions are running high.

One supportive coworker tells me to, "Write stuff down. Remember the details of these crazy events. This is a part of our history, and you should try to take it in as if making a record for future reference, like a history book."

She also suggests I take pictures — not of patients in an intrusive or inappropriate way, of course, but in a show-your-kids-how-crazy-things were sort of way. I'm not much of a selfie person, but I guess a few pictures of myself in PPE wouldn't hurt to take. This will later be the first seed planted that would grow into this book, even though I had zero intentions of a manuscript at the time (or ever, really).

My heart races as I answer the phone call from Employee Health that day at 9 a.m. I am still awaiting the patient's hepatitis results and thinking I could be in for a big life change.

Once I learn that the patient was negative for hepatitis, I breathe a huge sigh of relief. I won't have to try to quickly arrange for hepatitis treatment and all the chaos it entails.

Now I'm only left to wonder if the needlestick could have caused me to contract NOVA.

One thing at a time. I'll probably never even show any symptoms anyway. It's beyond my control; don't get consumed by that worry.

My home area isn't nearly as bad as Detroit and its surrounding cities at this point, but we also have been really behind in testing. I know from a local ER doctor that the testing criteria is so strict to be able to conserve the tests for the worst of the worst, making the numbers here not completely accurate.

Results on local tests are taking eight or more days to come back because they have to be sent to another city to get results, where there is a backlog of tests waiting to be run.

Healthcare workers will become high on the list to qualify for a test, but at this particular time, healthcare workers don't get tested unless they develop symptoms.

At the present time I have not been tested, but I am hopeful that the antibody test becomes available to me soon. This test basically shows if a person had the virus at some point, as the test would look for antibodies (your body makes these when it fights a particular infection).

At least at that point you could feel a slight relief that you now have some sort of immunity to the virus. There is some talk of catching it again (quite rare and may require the virus to mutate), but knowing you have the antibodies would still provide some comfort.

We were still testing only those who had traveled internationally in some of the hospitals, which wasn't the right thing to do given the community spread, but it was the starting point for conserving tests.

Later that day, I received a phone call from the director of the Detroit hospital, who thanked me again for my service. He told me how so many people told him that I was beyond helpful and heroic.

While I was happy to hear that, the situation was so grim that it is impossible to feel pleased with myself. He added that there's still a huge need at that facility.

He certainly wasn't pressuring me to come back, but telling me they would be grateful for any time, day or shift I felt up to working. I tell him that at that point that I am taking things one day at a time and not making any decisions, but would be in touch.

It takes a lot of prayer, my first yoga workout in years, hugs from my immediate family and crying to praise and worship music before I finally feel like I'm not about to have a panic attack on Friday afternoon.

Remember I'm still a wife and mother dealing with a lot at home, plus I'm extremely sleep-deprived.

Rejuvenated by another day away from the nightmare I experienced, I feel like I should go and help for one more day, knowing the weekends can be hard to cover.

The good friend I had decompressed to on my commute home before said it best when she said, "Don't you think if you decided to go back that you would feel more prepared since you now know what it's really like? Maybe you've already seen the worst?"

She is probably right, and I'm encouraged by that. My other shifts had been recently canceled, so I was available to help. I text the director, committing to 12 hours on Saturday.

Then I text the friend I had stayed with to verify she didn't have her kids so I could arrange to stay with her. She quickly calls me, which is a little unusual, and tells me I can't come.

Her children are back in her home because her ex-husband has tested positive for NOVA!

My heart sinks as I think about the other NOVA-positive patients I've seen.

Could this happen to him, too? No, it won't. He's one of the younger and very healthy people to have it. He will be fine. Just like I would be ... right?

He officially became the first person I know personally to be diagnosed with it. I'm worried for her and her children. She is an educated Advanced Practice Registered Nurse and knows that her children will be fine, and even considers it like an immunization for them. He has flu-like symptoms of fever, aches and lethargy, but she thinks he will be fine because his breathing is not an issue at all.

She also assures me that there's no way I would've caught anything from the night I spent in her home because the children's father had felt a little sick before the kids arrived. They hadn't been together in days previously, so he had it first — not the kids.

She is super calm about it all and seemingly not worried about whether she will get sick from the high likelihood that it is in her home.

Now I've committed to commute more than 200 miles to work a 12-hour shift under the most stressful conditions I've ever experienced.

I've also got to get up at 4:30 a.m. to make it to work on time on Saturday. I know I'm called to do this, and I can sleep later. Thanks to having a toddler, it wasn't all that long ago that I was waking up frequently throughout the night and I'm used to running on empty anyway. I know I will have plenty of endorphins to carry me through.

This is getting tough on my older children, who cry knowing they won't see me for more than a day and want me there with them at night just as much as I want to be with them.

It tears at a mother's heart strings to have her children cry because they miss her.

I'm not sure how long I can continue to help in this crisis, but at the same time feel called to help and almost feel guilty walking away from it.

CHAPTER 10

Saturday, 4:30 a.m.

I put on another set of old clothes from the bottom of my drawer, worn-out shoes and coat, and head out with a garbage bag of belongings like a hobo. This time, I remembered to pack a second pair of underwear, bra and socks for after the shower, shampoo and soap too, so that's a little comfort. I'm a fast learner.

It's not even 5 a.m. yet, and it's pitch black and foggy out. I can't even see one star in the sky through the fog. The road is completely empty, and I'm struck with the thought that everything looks like a ghost town.

I don't see a single car on the road for more than 45 minutes of driving through areas that are normally well populated. Maybe it's my brain, working overtime processing all that I saw during my last shift in Detroit and gearing itself up for another day full of facing the unknown, but as I look around me, it really does resemble a scene from the TV show "The Walking Dead."

I'm struck funny by the thought that I could probably be driving 100 mph right now and a police officer wouldn't even want to pull me over.

This thing — whatever you want to call it — is scary enough that the entire *world* is shut down right now.

Would anyone risk transmission for a simple speeding ticket? Doubtful. And even if I *did* get pulled over, I bet I could talk my way out of it.

Tempting... but I keep it under control. No use adding even more risk and stress to my day when it hasn't even really begun yet. That, and the fog is so dense that it's just not safe.

I am pretty wired for not having slept well in the past four days, but also think some caffeine will probably come in handy on the ride. Anyone who knows me, knows that I love a handcrafted latte, and I tell myself I deserve a little self-care at this point.

I rarely drink caffeine but when I pull into Starbucks, I order the fully caffeinated nitro cold brew, because it just seems right. No time like the present to try this drink my friends told me about! I had avoided it in the past because I didn't want to deal with the effects of the caffeine.

I am right: It is my source of happiness for the rest of the commute, combined with my anthem of hope-filled songs.

I arrive around 6:40 a.m., reinforced in equal parts from the caffeine and the small bit of familiarity that comes with entering a hospital for the second time. I stop to notice all the yellow "CAUTION: DO NOT ENTER" tape blocking off the other entrances that are normally used for different departments.

How did I not even notice that before?

I'm wearing a mask today and confidently flash my badge and announce my presence to the screeners as if I've been working there for years. It's a far departure from my entry a few days ago.

Once I've changed into scrubs, I find the CRNA who was overseeing the vented patients in the ORs and in the PACU (post-op unit) overnight.

He is a friend of mine from my community who answered the call to help as well after I assured him of proper PPE, so the conversation is comfortable and easy.

He gives me a report on all of the patients and tells me the night was pretty uneventful, other than one patient. This sounds miles different than my experience; my friend is maintaining, not admitting new patients.

Good. I can do this. I've already seen a kind of worst-case scenario, and it can only improve from here, right? Yeah. This will be a good day!

He gives me the highlights, which includes that the hospital has obtained sufficient IV sedation meds, which was one of my big fears on Wednesday. His biggest concern is that there is one patient in the PACU who had struggled through the night despite receiving maximum levels of oxygen and other ventilation therapies.

Turning patients prone (face-down onto their abdomen and chest) has shown to help these last-ditch-effort patients, as it stimulates blood flow to different parts of the lungs based on gravity, which essentially leads to a better balance of oxygen in the lungs and blood. I note that this particular patient was turned prone around 4 a.m.

I'm relieved to find a bit of order has settled in among such a chaotic scene from just three days ago. All of the patients in the ORs are now situated with monitors facing the windows of the OR, so by standing outside the room on a nearby step stool, I can assess everyone's vital signs and see their ventilators and settings.

I will see if any problems arise on the screens, as the alarms alert with bright, flashing lights and loud beeps.

Smart thinking, whoever did this.

This is great because it saves me from entering the room more than necessary and risking potential exposure. It can also save precious PPE, as I won't have to go into a room when things are status quo.

I first assess everyone from the window and have a peaked interest for the two that I settled into OR 14, including the one I had the needlestick injury working on. They are both now on a different mode of ventilation than when I left them as they eventually tired out from the 30 breaths a minute they presented to me with.

The ventilators now do all of the work, instead of assisting. They are also on more oxygen and vent assistance such as pressure. The rooms are all dark, which seems dramatic and just like it is on TV, but all the LED lit monitors are easy to see that way so I don't adjust the lights.

Oh yeah, this is so much better. This shift is going to be so much easier. It's actually pretty calm and quiet around here. Nothing like last time.

Sun is pouring through the windows all around me, giving an upbeat feel to my surroundings that I didn't experience on the last shift.

However false the sense of security and calmness it provides, it makes me smile behind my tight-fitting N95.

I talk to the night shift RNs about what kind of care the patients are receiving as their treatment regimen. It does include getting Hydroxychloroquine with Azithromycin, as I heard the President mention days earlier, crushed and put into their stomachs via a tube twice a day.

I had heard the Hydroxychloroquine was potentially difficult to obtain as people hoarded it for themselves in an attempt to prevent them from succumbing to NOVA. The drug is commonly prescribed for conditions such as lupus, and millions of Americans have legitimate prescriptions for it. I'm glad this hospital is able to get it for our patients.

Then the day shift RNs report for duty and they all look so young; maybe 25 at the oldest. I smile again behind my mask, thinking how brave they all are. I certainly didn't have to face a time like this when I was a young RN, and I know I had moments of being afraid even then.

They don't seem nervous at all. They almost seem calm and like this is any other day. I start to think back to my college biology and psychology classes, and wonder if their brains have even fully developed yet.

I remember being in my early 20s and feeling invincible in a way that changes later.

I imagine this aspect can probably keep them feeling a little more calm than I am inside. To me this would be a time where some ignorance is bliss. I am beyond impressed by their courage, grit, knowledge, strength and compassion. They are some of the best nurses I have ever interacted with.

These day shift RNs have worked with NOVA patients in their normal ICU setting for most of the week and know a lot more about these patients than I do.

There is definitely a component of desensitization that occurs over time when dealing with this day in and day out. A usual ICU assignment for them is two patients, although they tell me that right now each RN has up to four vented NOVA patients and their support staff has increased in an attempt to help with this dangerous increase in responsibility.

They're open with me about the stresses of their new reality — it's difficult to keep an eye on all four patients, and that the usual charting has changed for the better drastically because the hospital is trying to simplify what they need to do, leaving more time for eyes on the patients instead of the computer to chart.

It's time to reassess every patient from the windows. It doesn't appear that anybody needs any immediate changes to their ventilators.

Their oxygen saturation levels are all acceptable. It's about 8 a.m. now, and the surgeon-turned NOVA ICU physician comes walking down the hall. She has a Nurse Practitioner (NP) with her as well. They are rounding on all the patients to assess how they are doing.

This is the same surgeon I was with in OR 14 a few days back when I had my needlestick injury. She probably won't recognize me though with how brief our interactions were, combined with the masks we all wear.

Again, she is a surgeon and not used to managing patients on ventilators. Usually if a surgeon's patient requires ICU care, they consult a hospitalist, intensivist or a pulmonologist to run the ventilator and internal organ care.

Everyone has their specialty in the medical field, and surgeons' skills and talents are best utilized, obviously, in the operating room. I imagine she feels overwhelmed with her newfound role as well.

I am grateful she is a physician who has stepped up to help. She didn't ask for this. She is working extremely hard, long and stressful hours to do what is necessary and there are so many instances like this around the world now.

There can be no criticism during a pandemic when people are faced with these unprecedented challenges. For this, I thank everyone who takes on additional risk to themselves to provide care where it is most needed.

I smile again, and this time, I can actually feel it reach my eyes. It's funny how fast and fierce a bond can form during times when we are the most stressed.

I glance quickly around the hall at our band of misfits: Just about everyone is a stranger to each other. Sure, we're all highly trained professionals, and great at what we do, but we're also so far removed from our daily routines that the greatest comfort we can find right now is in the fact that the person next to us is also learning on the fly.

We are our own little club of overwhelmed people, all doing our best, drawing from our experience and winging it as we go.

The attachment to these strangers is almost instant and so strong it's nearly palpable. I think back on the stories I've read about the military; how people who spend just a fraction of their lives together wind up keeping in touch for decades afterward.

We are, of course, a battalion completely different from our country's veterans, but as we gather in hospitals to fight this invisible enemy, I can't help but understand how extreme circumstances can draw people closer.

The surgeon tells me she is considering taking the patient in OR 11 bed one off of the ventilator and extubating him (removing his breathing tube) since he is improving.

This move would make the ventilator available for one of the many people in the ER who need it, or someone on the non-ICU NOVA floor who made a turn for the worse and needed a vent.

So great to think that some people do *get better.*

At first glance this sounds like great news, but I was also informed first thing this morning that the negative pressure air evacuation system is malfunctioning in ORs 11 and 12. This means that any time the door is opened, the air the patient exhales will contaminate everyone and everything in the hallway.

This is an area that includes close to 12 staff members including myself as we've learned the virus can live for three hours in the air.

The patient in question is still quite contagious despite his improvements, making this a concerning issue to all of us.

Right now, his breaths are contained inside the circuits (one-inch corrugated plastic tubing that delivers and receives breaths from the ventilator to the patient's breathing tube), so the lack of negative pressure air evacuation isn't currently much of an issue where I'm concerned, but once he's extubated, everyone is at risk.

I tell the surgeon that we have informed maintenance of the need to fix the negative pressure system and that they are heading over to do so, then suggest we wait to extubate the patient until the air system is fixed, as it shouldn't take very long.

While I'm having this conversation, a message flashes through my mind.

There is no rush in a pandemic.

It's something I have been told over and over again. I also tell the surgeon that everything I have read — and it's been a lot — says that when you think a patient is ready to come off the ventilator, it's best to wait another day. People look like they are doing well, then 12-24 hours later they can take a sudden turn for the worse and need to be reintubated, or even die suddenly.

I do not want any part in making rushed decisions that also put me at an increased risk of exposure. The surgeon understands my concerns, and moves on to tell me that she has spoken to the family of the other patient in OR 11, and they realize that any more care is futile.

The 88-year-old caucasian man is on maximum levels of blood pressure and ventilatory support, but his internal organs — including his kidneys, which filter waste from the body and make urine — have shut down. After 12 days of ventilation there isn't anything further we can do.

Not only does the virus cause prominent lung damage, but it wreaks havoc on multiple internal organs and causes blood clotting problems, too.

The surgeon adds that all of the patients on our floor are now officially a "no code." This means that if any of them were to go into cardiac arrest, our care team will not rush in to perform CPR or other usual life-saving measures.

This is a tough decision made but it tends to be not only risky to the healthcare team, but impractical in nature because these patients don't survive long-term once they go into cardiac arrest.

I remember the nursing supervisor telling me that two out of the three patients who coded on Wednesday didn't make it. In general, a lesser percentage survives than the snapshot of that one day.

But what if you're that one?

These decisions are so hard.

Next, she moves on to talk about the lady in the PACU who was turned prone overnight. She'd like us to flip her supine (on her back) after four hours (which is now!), and then prone again four hours later.

Wait, what?

I'm certain my face looks puzzled.

Fortified by spending one full day in this chaos plus having read obsessively on the topic, I speak up to tell her that I respectfully, but vehemently, disagree with this decision. In the ICU, the intensivists have kept these patients prone for 16 hours at a time, as I had read and discussed this protocol with one of the regular ICU nurses.

The process of turning a patient in this condition is as labor intensive as it is risky. It takes at least eight people to assist since the patient is essentially dead weight, and it's important to maintain the patient's body in alignment during a turn like this.

Later, there will be proning teams of CRNAs dedicated to flipping these patients as many are in need of this therapy.

Picture a human-sized Gumby, with his top half twisted and the bottom half just sort of spinning to catch up afterward ... it doesn't work like that in real life. The turn is done in two steps during which I count to 3, then everyone starts and adjusts the patient completely lateral (on their side).

Once everyone is comfortable there and all lines are situated, another 3 count leads to the full flip. This, all while I am holding the breathing tube in place and guarding it with my life, because if that comes out, the patient could die quickly and we are all at risk ... especially me, who's positioned at the head and would have to attempt to re-intubate without having the PAPR air purifier to utilize.

The patients also have so many lines, or IVs and arterial tubings, that can come out during the flip. Not only is it time consuming and difficult, it's also risky.

Moving them in this fashion can also stimulate the patient to make them require even more oxygen or have unstable blood pressure during the flip, which is bad for them. And to do this every four hours for who knows how long?

No. NO. NO! I'm not going down without a fight.

I tell the surgeon that when this particular woman was on her back, her oxygen saturation was in the 60s, which is basically incompatible with life. She nearly died a few hours ago and is just now kind of settling in.

She says she thinks we can suction secretions better if she is flipped supine on her back again.

Time to put my foot down. There are too many risks involved, both to us and the patient. I tell her we will not do it every four hours, and we eventually settle on eight-hour intervals, which means her first position change should come in a few hours from now, around noon.

The surgeon proceeds to survey the unit, asking me to make a few vent changes on the patients in other rooms.

Entering these rooms means donning all that hot, uncomfortable

PPE, and every time I go in it's nerve-wracking, and I just want to get out of there as fast as I can and touch as little as possible.

I try to prepare well, grabbing every piece of equipment I might need during the shift to have with me to take in the room, which will help me avoid an unnecessary trip into the fire. There are a lot of pieces to my anesthesia machine that require maintenance when used in this capacity since they are not meant for ventilation over this long of a period of time (most surgeries last two to three hours or less).

As I gear up for the shift ahead, I can't help but think that just a week ago, I was on vacation with my family in Florida. We are Disney World freaks and were blessed to be able to go.

We were having so much fun there, and our biggest concern in the world was if we would get a boarding pass for the hottest ride on the planet ... Star Wars: Rise of the Resistance at Hollywood Studios.

My husband's joy as we secured that upon park entry was Over. The. Top. ... To the point that I had to calm him down so as to not make the others around us jealous who didn't get a pass.

Experiencing that realistic new ride led me to have genuine emotions and feelings of fighting against the enemy and moments of fear.

But the ride ended and we were left feeling victorious. We were literally at the happiest place on earth, having an amazing time. What I wouldn't give to have those carefree days back!

Instead I'm here wondering if this crisis will ever end. Again, I have very real feelings of fear, but this ride won't come to a victorious quick stop.

Can we just go back to our happy place?

We were lucky to have gotten our trip in before all the travel restrictions hit, unlike a lot of my friends, who had to cancel theirs.

The world I know changed so fast to get to this point, but I know it won't change back to normal at the same speed. Chances are we will all have to adjust to a new normal.

We have to mourn the world we once knew.

Right now, I'm in a hospital I never even knew existed, functioning in a role I never intended, in another state.

I find myself frequently battling with a surgeon over differing opinions. I find myself fearful and fighting an invisible enemy … the virus.

I am now afraid to be at work, but know I need to be here in this place and time.

CHAPTER 11

Saturday, 9 a.m.

The RN and I are working on a patient in OR 13 when the phone rings.

This is immediately weird to me: No one has ever called into an OR from an outside line to check on a patient during surgery, which is my normal work setting. But then again, this is now an ICU, and each patient has been assigned a bed as if it were a normal unit with a secretary.

Weird is the new norm.

I answer the phone since I'm closest, and it's one of the patients' family members, so I hand the receiver to the RN. He asks the caller for a PIN (personal identification number) to be sure this person is allowed access to the patient's information.

It sounds like the woman on the line doesn't have a PIN. They talk for a few minutes.

After he hangs up, the RN tells me it was the patient's nephew's girlfriend on the phone, who is basically the next of kin at this point. She was calling to say that our patient's husband has just passed away due to NOVA — I believe in the same hospital on another unit — and the next family member in line is severely symptomatic and now hospitalized with NOVA.

The whole situation, much like everything I've witnessed in my time here, is so surreal. I again picture scenes from "The Walking Dead," where entire families are wiped out overnight.

How tragic to think that in this hospital alone, there are probably multiple stories like this. Many of the people who contracted the disease didn't live alone, so their family is also at risk of becoming ill and possibly critical.

I'm not at all familiar with Detroit housing, but if there are a lot of apartment complexes, I can picture how each person in the complex could unknowingly infect so many others, days or weeks before anyone even knew they were sick.

I see a few large apartment complexes right near the hospital. The incubation period is part of what is so scary about this disease: It can take up to 14 days before any symptoms arise, if they show at all.

In fact, most people will never even know they were indeed infected, let alone if they spread the virus to others. In that time, according to an epidemiologist, one person could have infected 59,000 people! (This is the result of multiple layers of people infecting others unknowingly, and the exponential, terrifying growth.)

It also hits home for me that almost all of the people who suffer from NOVA will die alone, away from loved ones and near only healthcare providers they don't know.

I find a small bit of comfort in knowing they are sedated and their brains are at peace during it all.

I don't want to die alone.

At the same time, I'm so sad for these people and scared for our future. This is one hospital. What about the others in the city? The state? Country? World? It's like staring into a black hole.

I'm just one person, able to handle just several patients at a time, for about 12 hours each shift. What about the hundreds of thousands of others out there?

I can't control the world, but I can do my best with what's in front of me right now. I shake my head to clear the negatives.

Keep pressing on with today. You're here to do a job.

As I am about to finish there, I am summoned to OR 11 to extubate the first guy — the younger man who was actually getting better.

Ughhhhh. Now!? The negative pressure still isn't fixed in there, and his roommate is about to die. This has "bad idea" written all over it.

I'm prepared to fight with the surgeon making these calls for my side to be heard.

I don't have to work with this surgeon in surgeries when/if the pandemic clears, and I'm going to respectfully fight for what is right. I'm almost stomping when I walk between the rooms.

When I get in there, I calmly ask her why we can't wait until the pressure system is fixed. I remind her that if we extubate now, the patient will be awake when his roommate dies, which is just as horrible as it sounds.

Also — and didn't I already argue this point this morning? — I don't want to rush to extubate someone just to have to potentially re-intubate them. It's a huge risk that can't be taken lightly.

I'm not sure how quickly the patients who get extubated too quickly crash and tire out in turn needing to be reintubated. Is it 5 minutes? An hour? 12 hours?

Only a few people in the hospital have been extubated, and one of the ICU CRNAs told me a lot of them need to be put back on the vent.

The surgeon politely tells me she hears my concerns but says we can't wait any longer. I am not the attending provider, so I have to proceed with her request.

I tried.

Wait. Is she about to just pull the tube?

"No, no, no. WAIT! Don't touch that!"

Please stay in your lane! I am the airway expert; that's why I'm here.

I call out into the hall to have a runner grab me the equipment I would need to re-intubate, as well as gather all the drugs I might need to have to put the tube back in. I am the one on the line to fix this patient if things go bad, not the surgeon.

Then I tell the nurse to leave the room. She doesn't need to be put at increased risk. Because of the risk of transmission, it's recommended that only the absolute necessary personnel be present during intubation and extubation.

She happily scoots outside, and fast.

First, we need to give this patient a trial run of breathing on his own without assistance from the ventilator. The surgeon is not familiar with this sort of thing, but I am an expert in knowing if a patient is ready to breathe on their own; it's a decision I make on my own all the time with all of my anesthetics.

I politely ask the surgeon to go have a seat and wait as I make ventilator adjustments. If this is happening, we certainly aren't going to rush it.

I tell her that once the tube is gone, I can't add the same type of pressure therapy the man has been on.

She nods as if to say she sees my point and takes a seat on a nearby stool to watch. She is respectful and kind to me and heeds to my expertise.

I turn off the ventilator and stare at all the metrics on the screen while he breathes without any assistance.

After a minute, the surgeon says, "See? He's fine."

What is this lady's rush? Has she had more nitro cold brew than I have today?

I tell her that no way is one minute enough time to see if this man can sustain breathing on his own. I need to assess his tidal volume (how deep each breath is in mL), his respiratory rate and his oxygen saturation.

I'm talking to the patient the entire time. This man's sedation has been off for some time now to allow him the strength he needs to make his best breathing efforts.

In my readily available mom voice — which is apparently the only voice I have today — I tell the patient, "You're doing really well. Do NOT touch the tube. I'm going to get that tube out, but you need to cooperate."

He nods in agreement and even musters a weak thumbs up.

I suction him a few more times to be sure his lungs are as clear as possible, warning him first of the stimulation. There's a chance his cough won't be strong enough to clear his secretions without his breathing tube, so I take advantage of the suction system to clear as much as I can first.

He seems to understand me, and I just picture what is going on in his mind.

He is in an unfamiliar place, staring up at three people in hazmat suits who sound muffled through all of their PPE.

I picture George McFly in "Back to the Future," waking up to his future son, Marty, in a similar suit, calling himself "Darth Vader from the planet Vulcan" in a distorted voice.

The room is dark and strangers are talking to him in a very serious tone, because it's essential he understands how crucial it is that he follow my instructions.

Good Lord, I would be terrified. Is he wondering if he's been abducted by aliens?

I give him a quick, gentle hand squeeze to try to make him feel more like a human and less like a rat in a scientist's cage.

The surgeon breaks in to ask me how much longer this is going to take.

There is. No rush. In a pandemic.

Whether she heard my thoughts or picked up on the serious look in my eyes that tells her my patience is wearing thin, when I tell her to sit for 5 minutes she complies, and we make note of the clock.

Part of me is hoping this patient doesn't tolerate the trial because of the risk he is once the tube is gone, but of course, I ultimately want him and everyone else to get better. I continue to reassure the patient that he is doing awesome … and he really is.

After 5 minutes the surgeon stands up again and says, "See? Let's do it."

I tell her to wait just a minute: We need to put on the mask over the patient's head that will be his new source of oxygen and suction his mouth and lungs one more time.

As I pull the tube, I do my best to cover his mouth with the oxygen mask in one motion to contain his breath as much as possible in this room that is not a negative pressure room at the moment.

I hold my own breath and pull the tube. I tell the young man that his voice is going to be really hoarse and ask him not to talk. Coughing generates so much aerosolized virus, but it's also crucial for a patient who has been on a ventilator for nine days as this one was. I step a few feet away just to try to lower my risk but still remain close enough to assess him and communicate.

I tell the man where he is, what day it is and what has been happening to him. He is absolutely shell shocked. I am thankful his sedation has blurred his memory of the nightmare he's been living.

He shakes his head in disbelief and closes his eyes; he's still very weak. Watching him process what he's just been through is surprisingly emotional.

I hope later once the effects of the medications are long gone, buried in his subconscious, he doesn't remember any of this.

He raises his arms to rub his face, but his arms have no strength in them, and fall to the bed like wet noodles shortly after his attempt. I tell him to rest and to try not to move too much. He manages to hoarsely mutter, "Call my wife."

"Yes. Absolutely!"

My heart is so happy to think that he at least remembers what is most important to him ... his long-term memory is there.

I set up a new monitoring system for him. I take a moment to silently cheer for the man on the bed in front of me — he is my first NOVA patient without a ventilator or breathing tube! — but I still need to be able to assess his breathing from the windows without a ventilator and the alarms that come with it.

I am feeling great about how well he seems to be doing with just an oxygen mask, but even so, I leave the intubation equipment there for the rest of my shift just in case.

I then listen in as the RN calls this patient's wife at home, feeling my heart surge with joy as I hear the wife shout, "Praise Jesus!" over and over again through her tears. The RN cries with her.

It is a special moment of hope and joy, and they have been few and far between around the hospital these days.

I smile, fighting back my own tears as I tell the RN it's OK to cry. I will never forget this moment.

It appears this woman will get her happy ending and the answers to her prayers. She hasn't been able to see her husband in nine days and has been left at home to imagine the worst of the worst was happening.

She wasn't far off.

CHAPTER 12

Saturday, 10 a.m.

How is it still only 10 a.m.? I feel like it should be noon already. Time is crawling so slowly today. My heart rate is so fast today; my breathing, too. It must be the Starbucks. Just relax. Everything is going fine.

I'm summoned to turn the lady in the PACU onto her back again. How did I know the attending doctor wouldn't be patient enough to wait for the eight-hour mark we agreed on? I tell her that as soon as we see the patient's oxygen levels dip below 90 percent, she's going back prone regardless of the four-hour frame she wants. I just know her oxygen saturation will drop, and I'm not waiting until her levels are in the 60 percent range to do it like was the case last night, because she could instantly have a lethal arrhythmia (deadly heart rhythm) at those levels, meaning certain death for her.

A friend of mine who was on night shift told me how he urged the NP to order the proning protocol and was met with resistance until the patient was on the brink of death. I prefer to learn from the past.

Seven staff members are present, garbed up and waiting on me to begin to turn her. I'm not looking forward to this once, let alone twice, which I know is my fate. I get all of her lines and tubes as organized as possible.

I hold her breathing tube like nothing I've ever held before. I count to 3 and we do the two-step turn.

To my relief, it goes very smoothly and I don't even have to disconnect her tube from the machine to open the breathing circuit, which makes me feel safer. Her breaths (and the virus contained in it) stay contained entirely in the circuit.

Now we fix her up so she's not laying on any tubing. We straighten her head to a more neutral position and prop it up a bit. I suction her tube quickly, because that was the whole reason for taking this risk to turn her again.

I know she will desaturate (her oxygen levels will drop) and go backward in her recovery, because she was about to die in this same position just six hours ago and she can't possibly be better now. She seems as though she is holding her oxygen levels for the five minutes I watch her, and I remind the nurse to suction her every time she is in the room.

"No, actually double it up. Suction twice as much as you normally would, and I'll do the same."

Crisis averted.

I'm learning to celebrate every victory here, no matter how small.

Just then, I am called to OR 13 because the surgeon wants me to re-intubate that patient. This sends chills down my spine.

Re-intubate? Why was her tube removed!? Did her sedation run out? Did she accidentally pull her own tube out if she got loose from restraints?

I'm going to have to intubate my first NOVA patient!

This is really going to make my heart race. I figured this moment would come, but not in this fashion.

She is not even close to being ready to come off the ventilator as far as her lung health and should not have been moving enough to pull her tube out. I'm almost angry as I run in, fully expecting a crashing (dying) patient without a tube at all.

I burst in the door asking her, "What happened?" Except when I get there, I see it's not an emergency at all. The patient's oxygen levels are OK, and the surgeon is sitting by her bed with her arms crossed.

She tells me that she thinks the patient's tube is "going bad" based on the gurgling sounds coming from her mouth around the tube. These are abnormal sounds for a secured tube. The surgeon has attempted to "fix it" multiple times by inflating the cuff of air that keeps air from escaping (basic troubleshooting 101), and she thinks it needs to be replaced.

I tell her I will investigate, I'm not just going to pull the tube and replace it and she says, "Do whatever you want; just make it right," and leaves.

I do not want to take this tube out if I can avoid it. It looks like she did attempt the first line tricks to fix it, and I mess with it for a while, then think of a plan of action in case I do need to replace it.

My heart is racing and pounding hard. The patient looks like she could be difficult to intubate based on the anatomy that I can visualize, and I am all alone here.

If I pull her tube, then struggle to get a new one in, she could die. These patients don't have any reserve to buy me time if I can't get it in.

I don't want to be the reason she dies. Also, I don't know where all the necessary equipment and drugs are, so it takes time to gather.

Here I am, alone in the dark and truly scared for basically the first time in my career as a CRNA. I start praying to God to help me with wisdom and peace while I fix this situation. I think of the famous, comforting Psalm 23:4 from the Bible.

Though I walk through the valley of the shadow of death, I will fear no evil, for you are with me, God.

I have never even been close to a valley of the shadow of death before, but this feels pretty close.

I trust my skills as a practitioner, but this situation is different. I decide to take everything down to better visualize the tube, since the nurses tape all sorts of stomach tubes and securing devices to it.

I deflate the cuff (the soft balloon that inflates between the patient's trachea and the end of the tube to contain all the breaths and keep air from escaping around it) and advance the tube to a level that would seem too deep based on normal guidelines, but is an easy, non-invasive, low-risk thing to try first.

Then I reinflate the cuff and assess her. It doesn't initially work. I place my ear an inch in front of her mouth to listen.

Ugh! It's still gurgling, and I do not like being so close to her mouth and this escaping air! Are my ears covered? Can I get NOVA through my ear?

No; that's probably silly. Now fix this breathing tube, fast.

She is squirming in the bed a little bit from this new stimulation, so I give her some extra sedation. I tell her I have to make some adjustments.

"I'm here to help you. Try to relax, you are doing fine."

"Fine" is an exaggeration. I'm not sure if she will ever make it off the ventilator, but there is no point in scaring her.

Calming her is the best thing for everyone right now.

I deflate the cuff again. The gurgles become louder, which is expected. Her oxygen levels drop as more air escapes, and her ventilator begins to wail its alarm because it senses a large leak ... BEEP! BEEP! BEEP! It is sensing that she isn't getting the proper breaths she needs now.

Be careful; don't let the tube come out. If she coughs or moves right now, it could easily come out. She could continue to desaturate and turn into a true emergency any second now!

The tube is kind of stuck, and I have to stick my finger far back in her throat to manipulate it further. I eventually get it to advance and reinflate the tube's cuff.

I position my ear right by her mouth and hear nothing. No more gurgles! My prayers are answered, and I'm so glad I didn't just listen to the surgeon and yank out the tube. Within the next two minutes, her ventilator stops its wailing and her oxygen levels stabilize.

I give her a little more sedation to calm her from that increased stimulation, and she falls back into a peaceful, sedated state.

I feel like I have dodged a bullet. My heart rate can come down any second now. I still haven't had to intubate one of these NOVA patients yet since they were all intubated in the ER at this facility by the time they got to me.

At the other facilities where I work, anesthesia has been called to place the tubes in a lot of patients, but luckily, that has not yet been my fate.

I've always criticized TV shows and movies for making every surgery scene occur in the dark. Yes, some surgeries are done in the dark if the procedure is done indirectly via some type of a scope. However, the majority of surgeries are done with regular lights, including additional super-bright overhead lights to give the best visualization.

Hollywood always just makes it dark to seem more dramatic. But every moment of this day in the patients' rooms was spent in the dark. I never questioned it, but looking back, it really did add to the drama as if there were a director filming.

Only in this scene, no one ever yells "Cut!"

The NP is still on the unit but the surgeon has left for a true emergency surgery at the other side of the OR, far away from the NOVA OR hall.

The surgeon is probably so happy to be back in her element. I can't wait to be back in mine! I want to be giving anesthesia and in control and dropping people off after surgery who are in no pain and to their families who are relieved that the surgery is over.

That is so rewarding — it's why I became a CRNA — but this is what is needed of me now.

It's 11:15 a.m and the lady who we had flipped in the PACU is desaturating (her oxygen levels are dropping). She is already in the mid 80s when she had been 97 percent in the previous position.

She was supposed to be supine for four hours, but as expected, she's not better. We didn't even get any secretions when we suctioned her. From that, we've learned that she truly needs to be prone and we gave her all the chances we could.

We need to gather the crew and quickly get her prone again ... which again is far from an easy or safe task.

After the flip, she takes a few minutes to stabilize, but we get her back in the mid 90s and I think she will at least survive through this shift now.

I reinforce to the NP that the patient must stay in this position for the next 16 hours, and he agrees now. Another mom voice score.

There is nothing more we can do for her if she starts to decline now. She is my most critical patient.

The NP is assessing ABGs (Arterial Blood Gas levels that tell how much oxygen and acidity is in the blood) and wants to make vent changes to everyone based on the readings.

He has asked me to decrease delivered oxygen levels and other therapies on multiple patients, which means multiple instances of donning and doffing the PPE and opening the doors.

Nearly every change to the vent I make causes the patient's vital signs to worsen and leads to a struggle to stabilize them again.

I then have to put them on significantly more oxygen and therapy than they were on before the change to get them to hopefully stabilize.

The battle is two steps forward, one step back.

Almost no one is getting better. I have a serious talk with him about being aggressive with vent changes.

I know he wants everyone better this second, but it's not going to happen. We need to pump the brakes and not put me and the patients in danger by being so aggressive.

These are unchartered waters for him, too: He's used to following up with patients before and after surgery. These people did not have surgery. I tell him "no one else is about to come off the vent in our unit" and we need to just slow down because each time the patient drops their levels of oxygen, there's a risk they won't come back from it.

He agrees, and we decide not to try to wean anyone for a while.

Can't say we didn't try, but now we need to practice patience. They just need to rest and hope the Hydroxychloroquine, Azithromax and their bodies' resolve heals them.

He tells me that around the hospital, 70 percent of the vented patients are going to die. I think of the people in our unit. I don't know their fate of course, but I think that number is pretty close to accurate on our floor.

This week was during the crescendo of the surge of admissions, but I later heard of multiple cases where people were on the vent for well over two weeks, all the while knocking on death's door.

The patients were receiving every medication, supply and therapy possible to try to pull them through, in the end finding it to be futile on most occasions.

The cost of this care (it could be $1 million per vented patient), multiplied by the thousands of people affected in hospitals around the U.S. this way, is astronomical to say the least.

The hospitals, the government bailouts and financial help — this is going to hurt our country's economy for decades.

The nurse in OR 14 keeps saying that bed 1 is "trying to meet Jesus today," and I can't help but think that I was the one to settle her in just three days ago, talking to her until her sedation was fully effective. As ICU nurses, we have seen our share of death ... but never like this.

Never multiple patients, multiple times a day.

This is going to leave its mark on healthcare providers in an unprecedented way. Not only are healthcare workers becoming physically ill, the mental toll cannot be ignored.

I hope those young nurses can stick this out. I hope they don't leave the field of healthcare altogether after this. I wouldn't blame some of them ... the stories I hear from the ICU nurses are awful in regard to this crisis.

Especially for those first days of "the surge." ... I probably would've been crying at work, especially at that age.

This disease is relentless.

The NP also tells me that he is convinced he has or had NOVA, and like the CRNA the other night, adds, "We all will have it."

Neither of them were even poked with a "probable" NOVA patient's needle and they are convinced. I doubt I'll ever know if I had it.

I don't know the truth to this, but keep hoping that I do have or have already had it, that my course was mild, and that I don't suffer as these worst cases are.

I pray that I already have some immunity. He talks about how he can't sleep at night and wonders about every little cough, and I can relate.

I don't have a cough but everytime I think about my breathing, I question *Is it labored?* I cough a few times a day and think it has to be from wearing the N95 all day and feeling dry.

This isn't really what we thought about when entering the nursing field — putting ourselves in danger and worrying about our families — but it is our reality. Someone has to care for these people.

I wear a N95 respirator continuously, even when not in with the patients, for some sort of peace of mind.

All through the shift I think, *Am I having difficulty breathing? Am I coming down with this? No, this is just a little anxiety right? Anxiety is normal for this situation right?*

I try to assure myself that I am normal. I also rationalize my increased heart rate is because of the fully caffeinated coffee I bought on the morning commute.

You're fine. You don't have NOVA ... well even if you do, you're going to be fine with it. Oh and note to self ... you cannot handle a nitro coffee ever again. You're just stressed, and that's OK.

Right?

I go to the end of the hall where the hospital has stocked cases of bottled water for us to drink. I am thirsty and dehydrated from the mask.

I stop myself as I bring the water up to my masked mouth ... the N95 and outer mask are basically another appendage to me now; they never come off.

Here is where I get silly again, and start to think about a funny video I saw making fun of the Star Wars Stormtroopers who always wear the helmet that covers their face. They tried to drink through their masks too, and it didn't go well.

I walk around the corner, as if I can escape the contaminated air and carefully remove my mask for a drink ... and end up chugging the entire bottle.

This isn't an easy process (leaving and taking down two masks) so I'm going to down a whole bottle when I do take the time to drink.

This is when I realize how the tight N95 is really bothersome. There are deep indentations around my nose and mouth, and my whole face itches.

I want to clean my hands and just go to town itching my face while the mask is off.

Would touching my face be too risky though? Even with clean hands? Anyone would be breathing fast in these conditions. You are going to be fine; now take a deep breath and get it together. You're wired from that caffeine; that water is going to help. These people need us. We can handle anything that comes at us. You've always been competent, and you're prepared for this, too. It's just new.

And terrifying.

CHAPTER 13

Saturday, 12:30 p.m.

Our elderly man in OR 11 is about to pass away. No visitors, no family: Alone. ... but yet not alone, because the gentleman in the same room is awake and facing him. Since we are in an operating room, I know we have sterile drapes (opaque, blue, heavy paper made to separate the sterile operating field from anesthesia) to put up as we do for every surgery to make a sterile field.

I ask the OR staff runners to get two IV poles and drapes, and partition off the room so he can't see his roommate. It is dark in there, but their beds are facing one another.

In a normal ICU, there is one patient per room, so this is a non issue. However, with all the makeshift units across the world, I'm sure this situation happens multiple times a day.

Maybe he's too confused to realize what is going on across the room.

I hope. How terrible that I'm hoping a patient is confused!? Or at least that he won't remember it.

We just watch the monitors from the window. We are not in the room with him, as sadly there is nothing more we can do for him anyway. I say a silent prayer for this man and his family.

It is an uneventful death, lacking TV drama as we don't perform

CPR. His blood pressure and heart rate slowly fall, and after about two minutes there is no more blood flow, and he is officially dead.

I get especially sad when I think about his family mourning this loss from afar. Dying alone has to be harder on the family that wants to be there with him and can't be.

Are there even funerals or services for the deceased right now? It's just so unfair.

He passes away completely comfortable and sedated, and I pray he had no fears.

It is the first death I've witnessed from NOVA, but it's definitely not the first in the hospital. I know this man will be another statistic reported to everyone on the news in the next 24 hours. OR 11 has had a lot of action today.

A staff member tells me that the extubated man in OR 11 wants to go home; she asks me if that's possible. I tell her when someone wants to leave AMA (against medical advice), they can.

However, he in particular is way too weak. Remember the wet noodle arms? There's no way he can get up and walk out of the hospital no matter how hard he tries.

Not today.

After some education from his nurse, she thinks he understands he can't do that now. He has been on so much sedation over the last week that confusion is almost expected.

I know he is breathing OK, so there's nothing further I can do to help him. I suggest to the RN that we turn on the lights to orient him.

Imagine waking up in an operating room, except there's no one in there with you and it's a little dark. It must be so disorienting.

It's 3 p.m., and I am in need of nourishment. I take a break in the CRNA lounge, even though I don't know the people at this facility. There are a few CRNAs assigned to do the emergency anesthetics and cover the labor and delivery unit for epidurals and C-sections.

They are unfamiliar with the NOVA unit but are curious about it and supportive of me.

There are a few others in the lounge who are assigned to the ICUs and other NOVA vent units. One CRNA asks if he can come with me to see what it's like because he will be working the NOVA OR unit tomorrow for the first time.

After this late lunch, we head through the closed double doors of the NOVA OR. As if it's not unnerving enough stepping back through those doors knowing what's on the other side, each one is covered with bright yellow caution signs.

I learn that this CRNA is currently working for the hospital in a role which includes responding to rapid response calls throughout the hospital, and those typically mean a patient needs to be emergently intubated.

He is motivated to see what kind of vent and patient care details he will be responsible for tomorrow. I would do the same thing if I was in his shoes. It's always better to be prepared: I didn't really have a choice.

Should I tell him to skip the nitro coffee? Nah.

As he begins to gown up in PPE, I'm pointing out as much from the windows as possible to keep our time in the room brief. We are just about to enter an OR so I can show him my vent checks when his work phone rings.

It's the ER. He has to leave to intubate someone else, most likely a NOVA-related patient. He keeps his clean gown on and heads to the ER, as he will need it there.

We never do get a chance to reconnect.

I finally have a minute to breathe as we have agreed to stop making vent changes on the patients for now. I take the advice from one of the other CRNAs and take a walk. I give the nurses my number and wander around, checking out the rest of the NOVA units.

Was it really just a few days ago that I had a serious conversation with someone on social media about how overblown this whole thing is? I was trying to change his mind from one of pure economics devastating the country to that of the healthcare system.

I drew off what I had read about in Italy, and he questioned the validity of everything I said.

Here I am, walking through the middle of everything I told him would happen here. He almost had me convinced I was overblowing it.

Boy do I wish I had been wrong.

It makes me so angry to hear people in the general public talking about how "this is just another flu, and the flu is deadlier" and blah blah blah. I tell them that it's not about the mortality percentage, it's about the inability of our healthcare system to keep up with this demand.

This is not a "flu": We have NEVER seen anything like this. Influenza has never devastated the ICUs causing a need for more ventilators than ever imagined within a week or so. Influenza numbers are calculated over the course of a year; this has hit within a month.

I can't change people's minds who will never experience this first hand. I wish I could show these people what I see. I need to not waste my time with those kinds of people as they are unnecessarily draining to my psyche, and I need to focus on helping these critical patients.

As I walk through the ICU, I'm flooded with an extreme amount of noise pollution. I hear pumps beeping all over the large department combined with multiple types of alarms sounding.

BEEP BEEP HONK BEEP HONK.

Holy sensory overload! Worse than I ever remember.

The ICU ventilator alarms are unforgettable sounds that are still the same sounds as when I was an ICU nurse more than 10 years ago. I see every room has a vented patient and their IV pumps are outside of the glass doors, with extension tubing so long so they can keep the pumps in the hall.

Brilliant!

This helps keep room traffic down as the nurses can adjust rates on pumps without going in and contaminating the hallway air. Most of these rooms are not negative pressure rooms either, as hospitals typically only have only a handful of those types of rooms. (Maintenance quickly converted them all over ... shout out to that hardworking essential department, too).

It takes a lot of extra extension pieces to make the tubing long enough to reach from the hall to the patient, but it is a life saver! These pumps are constantly going off.

Each patient is on anywhere from three to seven IV meds on pumps. They need a lot of attention to keep the medication levels stocked, ready and safe.

Also, when the nurses are in with one of their patients (gowned and masked; the whole long routine), and another one of their patient's (they can have up to four) pumps are going off, another nurse can quickly help troubleshoot the alarm on the pump without gowning up.

This is so important because medication delivery stops when the pump is alarming. Imagine if this was their sedation, or life-saving blood pressure medication.

Another patient can quickly die if the pump is not tended to. Most of the time the alarm is an easy fix.

These nurses and assistants are amazing. The teamwork I see on this unit is inspirational. Even though they are all maxed out on stress, time and everything else imaginable, they still help each other without hesitation as much as possible.

I am touched by what I see even in brief snapshots.

I get an uneasy feeling when I walk through the step-down unit. These rooms have regular doors and no windows, so you can't assess a patient unless you are in the room with them.

The doors have to stay shut to keep airflow contained. There are more pumps in the halls and a lot of noises.

Whoa. This unit is the hardest place to work from what I've seen. I am so happy to be assigned to the OR once again.

I remember another CRNA telling me that there is a big problem in this unit with patients pulling out their breathing tubes.

They are on sedation and restrained, but sedation often needs to be titrated (adjusted) to a desired effect due to changing needs of patients. They also can wiggle their arms and work their hands to their mouths and tubes if they aren't sedated properly.

Most of them would likely be confused from sedation and a phenomenon called ICU psychosis, so they don't even know they are hurting themselves.

It's almost reflexive for them to want the tube out, but they can die from the repercussions if they aren't healthy enough to sustain their own breathing, or don't have someone skilled nearby to quickly replace it.

An entire floor of the hospital is dedicated to NOVA patients who require oxygen but are not yet at the critical point of needing a ventilator or intensive care. This floor has to have some very brave and attentive nurses, because those patients have the ability to decline fast at a moment's notice.

Throughout the hospital, frequent calls sound overhead for, "Anesthesia stat to room ..." This means one of those patients could potentially die without immediate help from the in-house CRNAs to intubate them. CRNAs are prepared for this with their traveling equipment and specialized PPE, such as the aforementioned PAPR system, that encloses the entire head and purifies their air.

One of the RNs tells me those "anesthesia stat" calls sound multiple times an hour. ... "Almost every 5 minutes, it seems."

As I make my way back to my ICU assignment, I pass the Labor and Delivery unit and get sad as I remember a story I heard on Wednesday. These pregnant women still have to have their babies amidst this crisis. They can't always stay home, and they don't have the ability to wait for the crisis to end to go into labor.

I had heard that NOVA has caused some pregnant women to develop a serious condition called preeclampsia that can cause preterm labor.

There was a patient the previous week who had to have an emergency C-section at approximately 31 weeks gestation (around two months premature) with a general anesthetic and breathing tube who was NOVA positive.

She had to stay on the ventilator for around three days and was close to being ready to come off of the vent.

I think of how sad it must be to be sedated for the first three days of your newborn's life. Being able to spend that time with each of my babies are some of my most precious and vivid memories of my entire life.

Still, she is a lucky one, one of the 30 percent to make it off the ventilator for now. It seems the younger ones are making up most of the 30 percent, which makes sense.

I'm thinking they will study the infant as there aren't many born to infected moms. If the baby has the virus, I wonder what this means long-term for the child.

I would think he or she would be OK since there were no deaths (at that time) under age 10, so that gives me hope.

I can't leave without checking on the patients in the unit I had started upstairs a few nights back. I was so curious how my guy who had been awake and cooperative with the TV was holding up, even though inside I knew it wasn't going to be good.

My heart sinks as I look in through the window of his room and see he is now completely ventilator dependent, fully sedated and not doing well.

He's on maximum oxygen, blood pressure support and needs a cooling blanket for his fever.

I'm glad the hospital has enough sedation now and wonder how bad it got that night after I left, but inside I'm thankful I wasn't there to witness it. The other two I admitted that night are also doing worse.

This merciless disease has just begun to take its toll, and the impending doom I feel is heavy.

I know some of them might recover … and pray for all of them. I never do find out how they fare.

CHAPTER 14

Saturday, 5 p.m.

Back on the unit, I sit down with the nurse from OR 14 as he looks at the ER census list. I imagine the place fresh out of a movie with patients doubled up in rooms because there are so many people in need of care.

It's almost like a holding tank in jail, where the door opens every so often and a new one comes in begging for help to breathe. It looks like there are a couple who have been admitted but are waiting on ICU beds and on travel ventilators until one opens somewhere else.

The medical administrators do frequent rounds to assess when the next vent will open up due to someone expiring or someone being favored enough to get better and not need it.

I know OR 11 will be filled soon after we get the postmortem care done and send the one man to the morgue.

The nurse and other staff members are about to take all the IVs and tubes out of him, and I ask them to turn on music for the awake younger man and to have someone distract him while it's being done. If we do it right, he will never know his roommate has passed.

The young nurse tunes the radio to some modern hip-hop per his request. The patient seems to like it. It seems odd to have club music on in a room while people are doing post-mortem care, but it's for another's benefit.

Meanwhile, there are at least 25 suspected NOVA patients on the ER census, their ages ranging from 23 to 102! If that centurion makes it out alive, it will be a miracle. All of their primary symptoms are pointing toward NOVA: Difficulty Breathing, Loss of Smell, Loss of Taste, New Onset cough.

A distinct, sudden loss of smell and or taste has been shown to sometimes be a first sign of the virus about to set in. The younger people on the list may not get critical enough to need a breathing tube; some may even be negative for the virus, but nonetheless the ER staff (including the ambulance staff) are so overwhelmed.

It's 6:30 p.m. and I am exhausted, but optimistic about getting to go home soon. My heart has been racing for most of the day: Thanks, Starbucks. My body has basically run a marathon with a heart rate that high for so many hours.

Well, no need to watch my calories today or tomorrow.

Things are going smoothly for the last 15 minutes of the shift, when a nurse shouts out from OR 11.

"Oh no! Help!"

The younger, awake man in OR 11 became confused and tried to get out of bed! As he lifted his legs up and over the side rails, he fell to the floor and hurt his knee.

His leg is bleeding, and he has a large cut. We can't just rush in; we have to be vigilant in donning our PPE. Luckily he seems OK; he's conscious and cooperative.

I need to know if he needs airway help now or not. He says he isn't hurting, and we reorient him. The usual course of action would be to send him to get a CT scan because no one was in there when he fell to see how hard the impact actually was.

However, he is still a highly contagious NOVA-positive patient who shouldn't be transported through the halls unless absolutely necessary.

Transporting him, combined with the logistics of how to handle him once in CT, means the whole scanner could be contaminated and potentially out of use for everyone for some time.

I know that he is stable and doesn't need any airway assistance. I don't think he is confused due to ineffective breathing and increased carbon dioxide levels, as I had assessed him regularly and he was good there.

The nurses call for a supervisor to attempt to get more staff to keep a continual eye on him. This could happen to any patient, at any time, in any hospital.

I sure hope he stays on the road to recovery and this doesn't affect him moving forward. Since the fall patient is under control, it's time to get back to the meticulous process of doffing my PPE.

I take off my shoe covers and hat and work through the final decontamination process. Every step is done carefully, complete with new gloves and sanitizer between steps.

The 3-minute phone sterilization is so important, as my baby might put anything in her mouth.

I shiver at the thought of my little angel putting her mouth on any NOVA-virus-containing object.

Finally it's time to head to the locker room for my try-to-hover shower. I brought my own soap this time and try to line up a new garbage bag to keep the contaminated stuff together. I also thought enough ahead this time around to bring a mask with me for my ER-commando-wet-hair-mad-dash out of the building.

Since I remembered a second pair of underwear, I won't have to go commando tonight. I'm learning.

I head to the elevator and push the button with my elbow. It's early enough tonight that I can leave through the main entrance and don't have to tour the ER! When the doors open, I sprint out of the building and don't stop until I reach my car.

What a long day; one that started with my 4:30 a.m. alarm.

CHAPTER 15

Saturday, 9:30 p.m.

I am so happy to see my family, but before I greet them, I first have to strip in the garage again and take another shower. My husband kept our kids up late so I could see and squeeze them. I cried my eyes out reading the homemade cards my older kids made me that said I was an angel and a hero and that they hoped I would feel better and happy again.

They realize their "Mumma" has not been happy. I try to shelter them from this scary reality and hide my stress from them, but this has been impossible to overlook.

Over the next few days, I regularly checked my sense of smell. I would stick my head in the refrigerator and was so relieved if I smelled a strong, foul scent. That's a first; happiness over gross smells.

But it was a sense of relief that I wasn't going to be heading to a testing center or the ER to get checked for the virus.

The nights were rough for a solid week after my last shift in Detroit. It was so hard to shut my brain down and not think about all that just had and would continue to occur, then wonder if this could be the fate of my own community.

I'd like to think that the sheer population and housing situation makes Detroit much more susceptible than my home area, but only time will tell.

My husband knows everything, but I'm careful to keep the worst of it from my children. They're so bright, and their brains are like sponges. Whether they communicate it or not, they're watching how their father and I respond to this pandemic, and it's important for us to set the right example.

When I want to cry and lie in bed, instead I try to be physically present for my family. Throughout this stressful time, we are all learning the difference between needs and wants, and how to sacrifice for a greater good and a common goal.

I'm proud that they will have seen their mother sacrifice for the good of others. I try to look for the silver linings whenever I can.

AFTERWORD

That next day, I sent a text to a CRNA in Detroit to make sure the younger man who fell out of bed was still OK, and that his injury wasn't a setback. I was thrilled to hear he was doing great and had been transferred out to a non-ICU floor.

I would later come to realize that cases like my awake and intubated man from the first day would happen on occasion. Most of those other awake people were those that were doing OK, but just not well enough to make it off the vent.

They were on the cusp of being ready, but this could take days and required brave and special patients and nurses to keep them awake.

I later learned that he was one of just 11 patients out of at least 70 to have made it off the ventilator after the week I worked ... so only around 15 percent of the patients.

Not great odds.

The others were either still fighting for their lives or had since passed away. Forty more patients — those who were never in need of ventilatory support — had been discharged.

So there is some hope, and the majority of the patients who die are either elderly or have significant underlying health problems.

The statistics in the news don't account for those fighting tooth and nail for weeks at a time; just the deaths. Those still locked in a battle for their lives cannot be overlooked, or counted as victories, as people attempt to compare the impact of NOVA to influenza.

Still, the toll this is taking on the healthcare system — which is also tasked with sustaining everyone else in the meantime — is unprecedented and an absolute war. It is a draining and dangerous nightmare to all staff involved.

I was only on the frontline of one of the worst NOVA battles in the United States for a few days.

These nurses and staff who brave this actual nightmare day in and day out, wearing their N95s and all the rest of the PPE all day, staring this monster in the face ... they deserve a medal of honor or something.

The signs from the community are nice and appreciated and bring a tear to my eye every time I see them.

But, these people are owed something more than just their salaries for their sacrifice. While a lot of people's biggest complaint these days is about being bored or the strain of working from home, the hospital workers risk a lot and work mandatory overtime for complete strangers; maybe even *your* family member.

I'm in no way trying to minimize the stress of home-schooling children or the loneliness of isolation: I'm living this, too.

We all have our struggles, and they are all real.

Shortly before this book was finished, the most tragic news came out of Detroit. The first death of a child diagnosed with NOVA in Michigan happened to a beautiful, seemingly healthy 5-year-old African American girl.

I have a 4-year-old and this information brought me to tears. Her parents are courageous first responders and my prayers and heart go out to them. She is one of three children under the age of 14 to succumb to the virus in the U.S. so far.

The article quote was spot-on when it said; "The numbers are low until it's your child."

Although my time spent in this particular hospital was only over the course of a few shifts, I personally have nothing but positive things to say about the organization. I am not an employee of the hospital and can't speak for their employees, but I was impressed.

A lot of this book may seem grim, but that's the nature of a pandemic. I really think the hospital did everything they could to prepare for this war.

First and foremost, I was so pleased with the level of readily available PPE. I was very impressed by how they rallied to get help and workers from other facilities to take the best care of their patients they could.

I was treated with such kindness and respect from everyone.

There were multiple occasions where high-level administrators went out of their way to shower us with genuine admiration and compliments.

They frequently checked in to see if there was anything they could do for us. I felt truly appreciated. They also supplied us with plenty of bottled water and regular meals and snacks to help keep us from having to leave the unit.

In addition, there were inspirational signs all around the hospital, encouraging us as providers.

There were so many brave people with whom I worked and have respect for beyond words. Multiple unsung heroes stepped up wherever help was needed; some even on a voluntary basis.

My profession also received some historic recognition as advanced practitioners when CMS (Centers for Medicare and Medicaid Services) suspended physician supervision requirements, which allows us to utilize all of our skills and practice at the top of our license.

This, in turn, allows us to have more autonomy and flexibility in utilizing our uniquely qualified skills and talents to help meet this huge demand on the healthcare system.

I've always been proud to be a CRNA, but never more than now. I know this book may make me come across as a scaredy cat, and while my emotions were actually those as described, I never lacked confidence in my skills. My training as a CRNA was wonderful, and I was able to hit the ground running.

I am a confident anesthesia provider. I knew my abilities were sufficient, and I knew I was fit for this task.

I relate the nerves to an athlete playing in a big game. Even Michael Jordan got nervous before his games, and it wasn't because he didn't think he was a good player.

This was a situation I had never encountered with so many unknowns and potential life-threatening consequences on the line for me and maybe even my family.

It's human nature to want to blame someone for this; however, this is the fault of a virus. This is a time for unity in the country, and we are all in this together.

I've seen first hand: This virus doesn't care about party lines, race, religion, income or anything else. There has been talk in Michigan and other places in America about the virus affecting a higher percentage of African Americans, which is definitely concerning, but I don't know how this translates worldwide when you consider it has killed tens of thousands of Chinese, Italian and other nationalities.

My point is that anyone can succumb to the virus: No one group is exempt.

As for me, I have no tolerance for divisiveness at this juncture of my life. I only want to hear about things that can make the circumstances better.

This situation is changing rapidly and will get worse before it gets better. I hope people will choose kindness and grace over fear and selfishness.

When people are scared, they unfortunately may lose their sense of logic and act in ways they may later regret.

After seeing the horrific war zone in the hospital, I have come to realize that my family and our health are to be cherished: All the rest is secondary. We can make more money in the aftermath, but our loved ones are precious and irreplaceable.

I went from being quite upset over all the money we had lost in stock market investments one week, to realizing how little that mattered the next.

I wish there was a happy ending to this story, one where the prince and princess live happily ever after (man, my Disney obsession really surfaced in this manuscript, didn't it), but we will have to wait a few months or even longer to see how this horrific tale ends.

Even when the NOVA hospital admissions slow down, my own employment will continue to be negatively affected — drastically so — because it will (and probably should) be a slow return to normal. I doubt the floodgates will open overnight, with the governor allowing all elective surgeries to proceed again. It will probably happen in phases. I personally will be severely underemployed, or unemployed, like so many others.

I do not minimize the effect this has had on our economy and in my own finances. I know businesses will go bankrupt and close left and right.

It is so sad, but it is important to remember that it is not our government's fault ... it is the fault of a virus. The President and legislative bodies all will benefit from getting the economy going again. We all have the same goal.

The extreme social distancing and stay-at-home orders were necessary to keep this Detroit situation from happening in my town and every other "Smalltown, USA." If you were lucky enough to be in an area that hasn't been majorly affected (yet), don't discredit the effect that the social distancing had to control it.

Your area was probably spared because of preventative measures. It worked in a lot of places and really flattened curves. Please continue to be patient through this, as everyone has experienced a life disruption—especially the frontline healthcare workers who have to deal with so much.

I had never thought of writing a book, EVER. But what started out as journaling for "our history" per a co-worker's suggestion, turned into therapy. I had so many people asking, "What was it really like there?" Sometimes, people need to know the harsh reality in order to grasp the true threat. It seems so far away for a lot of people, like it won't really affect them.

I'm hoping that this book can educate some on the harsh nightmare that could happen again in any city. Then I realized the public-interest side to it, and that by sharing my experience, I had the power to potentially influence even just one person to socially distance and do their part.

I know it is so hard to change people's minds, but that's not for me to dwell on.

It's not as a democrat or a republican, but as a *human* that I cringe to see people disobeying the stay-at-home orders from the governor.

These people may all feel healthy and never know the damage they have caused. They could've been the one to infect someone else's beloved grandmother, who is in turn put in the care of physicians who aren't prepared for this disease and then she is left to die alone.

We have a joke board at work and one says "Stay home unless you want to be intubated by a gynecologist."

I love my gynecologist, probably more than I should because he is an absolutely wonderful person and physician, but you don't want people working outside of their area of specialty, and that is the reality in a pandemic.

I haven't been within 6 feet of anyone, including my family (besides those under my own roof) since school was canceled in March. I miss them all dearly.

I want to hug my mother so tightly, but I don't. Both my parents and my in-laws want to hug and kiss their grandbabies who are growing so fast, but they can't.

I get quite disturbed by people who bring their small children to see their grandparents. It's not only against executive orders, it's irresponsible when people know better. They could be infecting others without knowing.

There are silver linings to this crisis, starting with increased family time. I could go on and on about slowing our lives down in general.

We are learning a lot, and I don't mean just always having a large stock of toilet paper on hand at home. I know my family is learning to live off of less. The children are also learning the huge difference between wants and needs.

I hope that our increased awareness of hand hygiene may even help suppress a few regular cold viruses, leaving us all a little healthier going forward.

If everyone works together to do what's right, we can give the healthcare system time to slow the spread and deal with the critical patients.

The creed is simple: If they don't live under the same roof as you, don't go within 6 feet of them. And don't go to the stores everyday because you're bored. Wait until you really need to go, then wear a mask.

By the time this comes out, maybe the restrictions are lifted and this advice is too late. But, it's definitely possible that another wave of this could hit and send us back into the stay-at-home orders, making them relevant again. Even better, maybe there's an antidote and the seriousness has declined.

Please pray for our healthcare workers and be kind to one another while we fight this war and await a vaccine. Let's all just do "The Next Right Thing."

This too shall pass.

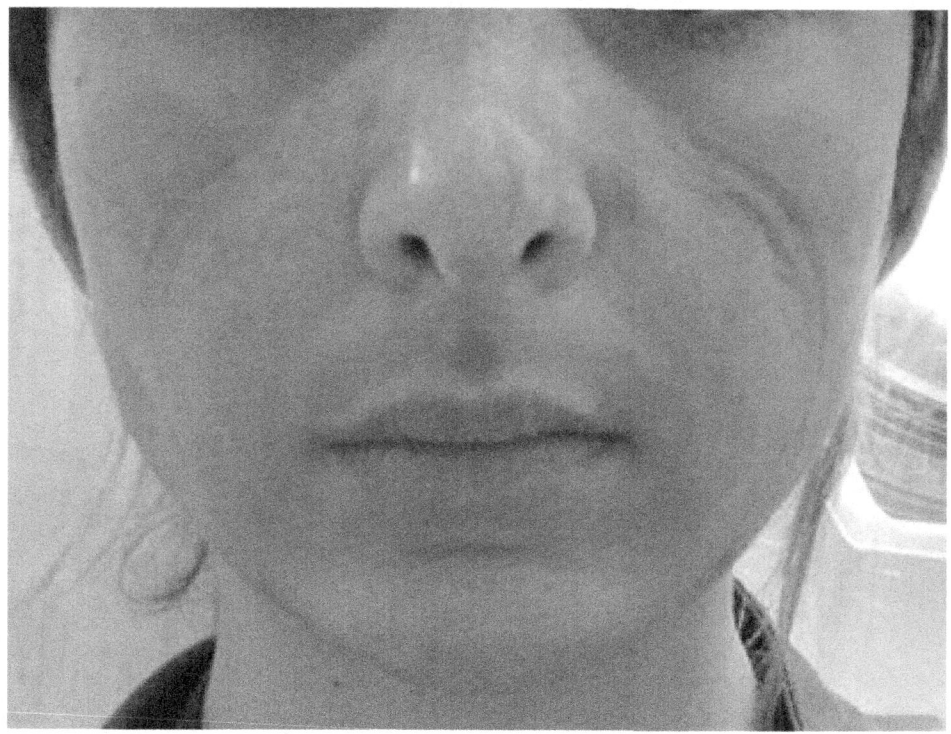

ABOUT THE AUTHOR

Tori Rose

Tori had never dreamed of writing a book until she experienced an unprecedented story that had to be told.

She is an experienced CRNA (Certified Registered Nurse Anesthetist) from the Midwest, and a wife and mother who thought her life was run of the mill until the viral pandemic calling was placed on her life.

STEPPING INTO THE STORM

Ever wonder what it's really like in the hospital for a patient or the healthcare workers during a viral pandemic? Family members aren't allowed in to see their loved ones, even in their last moments on earth. This book provides a true first-hand account of the harsh reality on the frontlines of such a battle. Real thoughts, experiences and fears of a healthcare provider putting herself at risk during the height of the viral surge, when the healthcare system was pushed to its breaking point. Some say it's all a hoax, but you will read actual chilling events from a CRNA who experienced it up close and all too personal in the epicenter of Michigan's novel virus hotspot. This fast, easy read will keep you wanting more as you feel you are there in the ICU, too. You will be scared, you will be moved as you get an inside look at something you hoped to never experience but always wondered about. You will know this virus is more than another flu after you step into the storm.

Made in the USA
Monee, IL
21 December 2020